Born for the Bear

A NOVEL BY

Annabelle Winters

Books by Annabelle Winters

The CURVES FOR SHEIKHS Series

Curves for the Sheikh
Flames for the Sheikh
Hostage for the Sheikh
Single for the Sheikh
Stockings for the Sheikh
Untouched for the Sheikh
Surrogate for the Sheikh
Stars for the Sheikh
Shelter for the Sheikh
Shared for the Sheikh
Assassin for the Sheikh
Privilege for the Sheikh
Ransomed for the Sheikh
Uncorked for the Sheikh
Haunted for the Sheikh
Grateful for the Sheikh
Mistletoe for the Sheikh
Fake for the Sheikh

The CURVES FOR SHIFTERS Series

Curves for the Dragon
Born for the Bear
Witch for the Wolf

BORN FOR THE BEAR

A NOVEL BY

ANNABELLE WINTERS

2019
RAINSHINE BOOKS
USA

COPYRIGHT NOTICE

BORN FOR THE BEAR

1
<u>DAMASCUS, SYRIA</u>

I wish I'd never been born.

Bismeeta Khalifa twisted her long black hair into a hasty bun and hurriedly pulled the top of her *hijab* back down before anyone saw her without the traditional Arab head covering. Well, it wasn't really her *hijab*. She'd stolen it from one of the other teachers' lockers. Her own black robe and head covering was a tattered mess—not that she could even find it. Once again she'd ripped her way through her clothes when *that* had happened. When she'd turned into . . . *that*.

"What is happening to me?" she whispered, staring out the window of the empty restroom as the footsteps outside thankfully moved past and faded into the distance. "Why am I cursed? What have I done to deserve this, Allah? Have I not lived my life as You wished? Was it wrong to forsake marriage and family-life and instead devote my time to the children of our war-torn country? Was that not my destiny? Did I violate some cosmic law by choosing to go my own way?"

She sighed as she gazed through the grimy windows of the school building and down at the schoolyard, which was not much more than a dusty sandpit with three craters the size of swimming pools neatly lined up at the far side. Craters from three bombs that had "mistakenly" missed their real targets—whatever those were. No one knew if the planes that had bombed the schoolyard were Russian, Saudi, Iranian, or American. Everyone and their grandmother was bombing Syria these days, it seemed. Target practice, maybe? Why not!

Bismeeta chuckled as she pulled at the bottom of her "borrowed" tunic. It was tight beneath her breasts, and she frowned as she wriggled her large bottom and tried to get a decent viewing angle in the cracked mirror. She sighed when she saw the pronounced panty-line showing through the black robe, which was about five sizes too small, it seemed.

A panty-line would be deemed too "provocative" if she was seen on the streets. She'd have to wait until it was pitch dark outside before she dared leave the school building.

Of course, when it got dark outside, there was a good chance she wouldn't be leaving the building as a human . . .

Bis gasped as she felt it move inside her like it was alive and listening, crouching there in the background. Her heart began to pound, and beads of sweat appeared on her smooth brown forehead as she stared at herself in the cracked mirror. Why was this happening? Was it because she'd looked at that flying beast in the eyes out in the desert? Because she'd dared to meet the gold-and-green gaze of what could only be the devil? Was she possessed by some evil now? Doomed to transform into an animal that slinked through the darkened alleyways of Damascus by night?

She clamped her eyes shut tight and swallowed hard, trying to push back the thoughts that had been pouring into her like it was a splintered part of her personality speaking directly to her messed-up brain. Yes, that was it. Her brain was messed-up. The years of listening to bombs drop like rainfall had finally taken their toll. Something had been shaken loose in her head, and after she and all those girls had been kidnapped as war-brides and sex-slaves, the loose-screw had simply fallen out and now she was completely insane. Her dream-world and real-world were indistinguishable.

"You claim you've seen a dragon, after all," she muttered as she opened her eyes again and spoke to her cracked reflection. "None of the other girls say they saw it. Half of them are still traumatized. Some of them had their eyes closed throughout the ordeal. The rest claim it was just some new kind of airplane that swooped down and killed our captors, tossing them around like ragdolls, burning them alive, even eating a few. *Eating* them! What kind of airplane eats people?!

For a moment Bis was furious at the girls for not supporting her story that yes, it was a *dragon* that had saved them! But she took a breath and did her best to release the anger. People see what they want to see, she told herself. They believe what they want to believe. How else to explain the madness of what is happening all around us—in Syria, Iraq, the Middle East . . . indeed, all over the damned world!

Again she heard footsteps outside the door and she froze. Her next class was about to start, and she needed to be calm and pleasant, optimistic and happy. After all, it had been her decision to return to Syria after finishing university in London and then landing a teaching job in Birmingham. She could have lived an easy life in England, but instead she'd traded in her jeans for a *hijab* and landed her big bottom back in Damascus with some idealistic notion that her place was here, that it was her responsibility to help, that she couldn't just leave it up to the United Nations or whichever country decided to send in a few soldiers or planes to combat what was happening here. She wanted to do something. To contribute. To help, dammit!

The footsteps were gone, and Bis grabbed her ears, opened her mouth wide, and let out a silent scream. There was so much energy inside her that it felt like a ticking timebomb, like she was primed to explode, do something drastic! She couldn't stand there in front of a group of children, put a smile on her round face, and then try to teach them English so they'd be better candidates as refugees when they got a chance to get the hell out! She just couldn't do it anymore! She wanted to do more. She needed to do more. She *had* to do more! Because . . . because . . .

Because you were born for it, came that hissing voice from inside her, making Bis almost throw up in panic. It was too real to be ignored. Too clear to be denied. *Born for this. Born for him.*

"Born for what?" she said, her brown eyes going wide as she realized she was actually talking back to this voice that was just a sign of a split personality or something. "Born for whom?"

The bear, came the response from inside her. *You*

were born for the bear. You are the only one who can save him. The dragon and his mate need you to find the bear. Bring him back to them. Have babies with him. Continue what has already been put into motion. The dragon and his mate cannot do it without you. You are the missing piece, Bismeeta. The missing piece.

2

So many missing pieces.

Bart the Bear blinked at the sandstone floor as he tried to put it all together. But there were too many missing pieces to form even the semblance of sense. It was like a jigsaw puzzle that had no picture on the box to even guide him. He pawed at the ground, blinking again as he stared at his massive paws that looked filthy, dried mud trapped between his toes, his claws scarred and chipped like he'd been trying to rip through concrete, stains of dark red that Bart didn't even want to think about.

Not that he could even remember what had happened over the past few months. Or had it been years?

He couldn't even remember the last time he'd been in human form, and judging by the way his fur smelled, it had been a while. A long while. Too damned long. He was all bear. All wild. All . . . trapped?!

With a roar he slammed his massive body against the titanium bars of the cage, feeling them bend and clang. But they didn't give. They didn't break. He wasn't strong enough.

The realization ripped through his bear, and he pawed at the sandstone floor again, his claws leaving long scratch marks as he prepared to rush the cage again. He could break through walls, knock down trees, flip over cars, trucks, and goddamn tanks when his bear was in control! He'd break through these bars soon enough. Then he'd find whoever put him here. Ask them some questions. Get to the bottom of whatever was happening here.

No questions, whispered his bear. *What are we, nerds? We don't ask questions. We don't give a shit about answers! We destroy and demolish, run rampage and roar loud, feed and fuck! I am in control here, weakling! Let me handle this!*

Bart grunted as he searched for the human inside him. The man was there, but he was buried deep. The bear was in control, like it had been in control for years, decades, forever perhaps.

He raised his snout and let out a mournful roar, a sense of despair washing over him, an overwhelming feeling of failure. He'd failed his parents, his crew, himself. He'd failed to be a good man, and now he was doomed to spend his days as an out-of-control beast. Why was he even still alive? Why hadn't they put him down yet? After all, if someone could put his bear into a cage, surely they could put him out of his misery just as easily.

Once more he rushed the cage walls, his heavy body bouncing off the bars as he felt pain shoot through him like he'd been electrocuted. There was something about the metal, he realized. A current of energy. Electricity? Magic? Who the hell knew? Bart wasn't a thinking man. He'd barely made it through high-school before the Army had given him an outlet for his aggression. Then John Benson had arrived on the scene, and he'd been put together with Adam Drake and Caleb the Wolf. Two men like him. Two military brothers. His crew. His goddamn *crew*!

Again he wailed, but this time Bart felt the man inside him reach out and try to seize control from the animal. The memories of that short time when Bart had felt like he was a part of something, like his life might have some purpose, like there might actually be some meaning to the madness of what he was . . . shit, those memories actually made him feel *good*! Feel like there was hope! Like maybe he didn't want to die just yet. Maybe there was something waiting for him . . . perhaps some*one* waiting for him.

Break these bars and find her, growled the bear from inside him as Bart cocked his furry head at the last thought. *Find her and claim her. Take her. It is our fate. She is our mate.*

"Who?" said Bart, blinking in surprise as he heard his own voice. How long had it been since he'd spoken out loud—spoken words and not just animal-sounds!

But the bear didn't answer, and once again Bart felt his body lurch forward, his rock-hard head smashing into the cage and making him see stars as the bars just rattled in delight at the stupidity of the beast.

"The beast is dumb as a rock," came a man's voice from the far side of the room. A strange accent, like it was a mix of Middle-Eastern and European. Old world in a way that reminded him of something, of someone. Adam Drake? No, this wasn't Adam. "Does it not realize it cannot break through its cage? These monsters are more stupid than I thought. We can do nothing with him. Have the wolf put him down."

Bart rose up on his hind legs, reaching up with his snout and sniffing for a scent. Now the smells of his surroundings came rushing in, and he panted in glee as he remembered that there were some good things about being an animal too. His bear's eyesight wasn't great, but its hearing and smell were unmatched. He could navigate through forest and river on a moon-less night with just those two senses guiding him.

Slowly a feeling of power drifted into him as he closed his dark brown eyes and sniffed the air again, his ears twitching as he slowly formed a mental picture of what was happening. He couldn't smell any trees or underbrush, no rivers or lakes, no lush greenery or soft mudbanks. The air was dry and hot, and the only scents he could pick up were that of barren sand and dry rock. He was in a desert, he realized as he took several deep breaths. He picked up the hint of an animal's scent, grunting when he realized it was just a rat from somewhere in the building where he was being held. Then he snorted and focused on the humans who were talking in the distance.

"He is from a strong, powerful bear bloodline," came another voice, a woman's whisper, low and guarded almost like she knew Bart could hear her. "His children will be powerful too. We might not be able to control him, but we might be able to control his offspring. It is worth a try. He stays alive. Besides, the wolf will not be able to put him down. Only a dragon can do that."

Every hair on Bart's thick neck stood up as he sensed how the man tensed up at the word dragon. He's a Shifter, Bart realized. A dragon Shifter! I'd recognize that smoky scent anywhere!

A chill ran through his bear as he realized that the woman was right: A dragon was pretty much the only thing Bart knew better than to go against. He'd seen Adam Drake as a dragon, and there was no going against all that fire and fury. Bart's bear knew a thing or two about rampaging, but you hadn't seen a rampage until you saw a dragon burn its way through a hundred acres of forest!

But even as the thought came, Bart felt the smoky scent disappear almost as if by magic. He could hear the man's breathing relax even as he heard the woman's heart beat a little faster, like she was using some of her energy to help calm him down, help control him . . . control his dragon.

"All right," the man said finally. "The bear lives. We can use him to seed the next generation of bear Shifters . . . beasts that will be loyal to me. Now Change him back to human form, please. I'd like to ask him some questions, and I detest conversing with an animal."

Bart felt the woman tense up again, and he shuddered and squinted as the bars of the cage glowed with a strange dark light. He felt the human inside him move, but there was no Change. He was still bear.

"It's no use," said the woman after a moment. "He's gone feral. I cannot Change him back. It would take too much power, and I am already using much of my power on you, Murad."

"Call me Sheikh, please," said the man. "Sheikh Murad."

He stepped closer to the cage, and finally he was close enough for Bart to see him clearly. Tall, wiry, with broad shoulders that looked smaller because they were pulled in tight, like wings that hadn't been stretched in decades. He had a meticulously groomed gray beard and long dark hair. Sunken cheekbones and a gaunt jawline. But those eyes . . . blazing gold eyes. Bart had seen those eyes before—at least one of those eyes!

"Yes, Sheikh," said the woman, and Bart blinked and squinted so he could make her out. She was a small woman, dressed in a dark red gown the shade of dried blood. Her lips were dark red, her eyes like little black beads that seemed to look right through him. There was magic in her, he knew. Dark magic.

"Feral," said Murad, peering at Bart like this was a zoo. "You mean wild. Berserk. Out of control. The animal is in full control, and it does as it pleases—which appears to be mostly breaking things."

Bart growled as he felt his bear nod in agreement. Breaking things sounded like a reasonable strategy. First the cage, then these two, and then perhaps that rat he'd sniffed earlier. He was hungry, and rat would do just fine as dessert after he ate these two skinny humans. Again he hurled himself at the bars, roaring in pain and anger as they tossed him back onto the sandstone floor once more.

"Yes," said the woman. "Feral. He needs to mate. It is the only way to Change him back to human. It is the only way to get the bear in him to give up control and allow the Change."

Murad nodded. "Because these creatures only mate in human form. All right. Good. So bring a few women here and toss them into his cage. Let the breeding process begin!"

The woman snorted, glancing over at Murad as Bart watched. "It is not so simple. He is more likely to eat a woman than mate with her. The Change will not happen with just any woman. It has to be his fated mate."

Murad swatted at the air, frowning scornfully as he turned to the witch. "There is no such thing as a fated mate. It was just a story invented centuries ago to control the sexual appetite of these shapeshifting monsters. Just a myth to keep them from mating with anyone and everyone they fancied."

"That is what I believed too," said the woman, lowering her voice again. "But how else can you explain the dragon finding us so quickly?"

"Magic," said Murad with a shrug. "You tracked them down to the South American rainforest with your magic, didn't you? The woman was pregnant with my grandchildren, and you used the blood connection to form a cosmic connection. My son must have found someone who could work the same magic."

The woman smiled, and Bart could sense a flash of anger in her mud-colored eyes. "There is no else who can work my magic. This was magic, yes, but a different kind. We cannot dismiss the legend of fated mates so easily."

Murad sighed and swatted at the air again as Bart imagined swatting his heavy front paw and cracking the asshole's skull open like a coconut. Coconuts were good fiber and healthy fat. Damn, he was hungry! What kind of bear fantasizes about eating coconuts?!

"Whatever," said Murad finally. "So then find his so-called fated mate and toss her into the cage with him. Doesn't matter to me, so long as we get this process moving along. It is hard to build a Shifter army without any Shifters besides that wolf and the few others we have managed to capture. You failed with Adam's pregnant mate, Magda. Do not fail me again."

Magda the witch took a long, slow breath, her eyes burning red once more. Bart stared at those eyes, a memory of a different set of red eyes coming back to him as his mind swirled. Red eyes like that, but on a wolf. On Caleb the wolf? Perhaps. He couldn't be sure, the memories were so hazy. But he'd definitely seen a wolf with red eyes before ending up in that cage. If it was Caleb, he'd kill that mangy piece of wolfshit!

Bart growled as he and his bear tried to make sense of the bits and pieces of information and memories bombarding him. Bart had always been the muscle-guy in an operation. All this thinking just made him angry! Shifter armies? Traitor wolves? Adam Drake? And from what this old bastard was saying, was he Adam's . . . Adam's *father*?! What the hell? No wonder Adam never spoke of the guy! He was a goddamn lunatic!

"Yes, Sheikh," she said finally, her voice coming like the hiss of a snake. "Though if you do not be-

lieve in fated mates, then perhaps you might consider fathering another child. Another dragon. The
dragon is the most powerful Shifter, and if you sire
an army of dragons, we will not need to bother with
bears and wolves."

"Father another dragon," muttered Murad, shaking his head, his eyes gleaming gold. "With whom?
You? Hah!" He shook his head again. "No. I am the
last dragon, and I like it that way. Besides, bears,
wolves, and the other Shifter animals all have their
special qualities. They are also easier to control than
dragons."

Magda snorted, glancing at Bart and then back at
Murad. "None of these creatures are easy to control.
We got lucky that my magic worked on the wolf." She
paused as if wondering if she should keep going. "Also,
you are not the last dragon, Sheikh. Adam Drake is
the last dragon, and when his mate gives birth, neither of you will be the only dragons left on Earth. You
may want to think about—"

"I will decide what to think about, thank you very
much, Magda. Do not forget your place in this, witch.
I will deal with the issue of my son and his pregnant
mate when the time comes. Your priority is to find
this bear a woman so we can get moving on building my army."

Bart watched as Murad's black robe glowed with
the same dark light that he'd seen flash from the

bars of his cage when he'd tried to break through. Murad's robe was infused with the witch's magic, Bart realized. Was that what the witch had meant when she said she needed to use some of her power on him? To keep him from Changing? Why? Did Adam's father not *want* to Change? Did he not have control over his own dragon?! As for Adam having a mate who was pregnant . . . was that true?! Shit, he'd clearly missed a lot while lost to his bear in the South American rainforest.

Magda the witch sighed, her red eyes darting to the bear before she gazed past him. "Finding the bear's mate is not so easy. I have no blood connection to her, no way to use magic to track her down. We will simply need to wait."

"Wait?" said Murad. "Wait for what?"

"The universe draws fated mates together," said the witch. "And so his woman—whoever she is—is on a path towards him. All we need to do is wait."

"I said it once and I say it again: Fated mates are a myth. This beast will take whatever we serve him. You say he needs to mate, yes? Then bring him some women. I cannot imagine he will be too discerning. Worst case he will eat the ones he does not want to fuck. We do need to feed him anyway, don't we?"

Magda flashed him another look of red anger, and Bart frowned as he wondered what hold Murad had on the witch. Why was she working for him? Clearly they weren't lovers. Was it money? But if she was a witch, couldn't she just . . . *conjure* up some money? Who knew. The details of magic were above Bart's pay grade. He was brute labor, just a grunt, the muscle not the brains. At least that's what Caleb and Adam used to say when the three of them were giving each other shit, talking tough, testing each other like men did.

A smile came to the bear's face as he retreated to the back corner of the cage and watched Murad and Magda leave the sprawling empty room. Damn, he missed that feeling of being part of a crew, part of a pack, having friends, brothers, a purpose, a goddamn mission!

I also miss that feeling of being human, he thought as he stared down at his stained paws, his chipped claws, the matted fur on his massive shoulders and haunches. Was the witch right about him? Was taking a mate the only way for Bart the man to find his way back? To gain control of his bear?

Only one thing to do, Bart thought as he finally settled down on his haunches and stared into empty space. Wait. Just like the witch said, there's nothing to do but wait.

3

I cannot wait any longer, Bis thought as she let herself out of the empty school building and hurried down the street in her grossly undersized clothes. The sun had just set, but it was still light outside. She'd wanted to wait until darkness fell, but she was too scared of what might happen. She was too scared of *that* happening . . .

She'd tried to avoid the other teachers as much as possible during the day, but she'd definitely noticed a couple of them glancing at how tight her clothes were. Maybe they simply thought her ass was getting bigger, she told herself, smiling and shaking her head. Truth was, she *had* gotten heavier over the past few weeks. She'd never been a small woman, but after that incident with the kidnapping and the dragon, her eating had gotten out of control!

Bismeeta's face lit up in a smile as she sniffed the air and picked up the familiar aroma that wafted from the battered chimney of a little pastry shop—the only structure left standing on a bombed-out street near where she lived. Could she stop? Did she dare walk in there in her undersized robe, her panty-line showing like she was a woman of the night?

She narrowed her eyes as the lights of the pastry-shop came into view. It was empty—just the old, mostly blind owner hunched over behind the counter, culling the unsold items from the day. She knew the old man. At the end of each day he pulled all the unsold items and wrapped them up for delivery to the local schools, including hers. He claimed that he only did it because he had a strict policy of only selling pastries baked the same day, but Bis knew better. It was just the old man's way of diverting attention from his good deed.

Bis felt a surge of warmth in her breast as she remembered that even in the midst of all this death and misery there were people who did what they could to help, people who gave a damn, people who cared about others. This was why she'd returned, wasn't it? Because she knew she could help, knew she could contribute, knew she could make a difference . . . that she was *born* to make a difference! She wasn't sure how or when or even why. But she knew what she felt. It felt like . . . fate. Destiny. Meant to be. Like she was on a path ordained by the universe, and she had no choice but to walk that path.

"Hello!" she called out as she followed the footpath to the pastry shop, knocking twice on the window pane and walking in with a beaming smile for the kind old man. "What treats are the kids getting tomorrow?"

"Bismeeta!" the old owner said, his cataract-glazed eyes lighting up as he raised his head from behind the counter. "Ah, the children will have almond brittle, camel-milk cookies, and brown-sugar cakes for breakfast tomorrow. Plenty left over. Here. Try one!"

Bis took the sample without a moment's hesitation, ignoring the bit of guilt she felt for eating into what was going to be shipped off to hungry kids the next morning. Everything was delicious, but when Bis glanced down at the counter, she realized that there was so much still left over that the man must have barely sold a thing all day!

She took a breath as she wiped her mouth, feeling a rush of shame when she remembered she didn't have any money on her. She opened her mouth to thank him again—and perhaps to suggest that he didn't need to donate so much if it was a hardship; but the sound of the bell above the front door startled her.

"Well, well, well," came a man's voice just before she had time to turn. "Are you running a brothel now, old man?"

Bis felt something move inside her as she turned to meet the bloodshot eyes of three men, their beards ragged and long, their tunics stained and smelly. Although alcohol was forbidden for Muslims, clearly these men had been imbibing in the fermented cactus liquor that was popular in underground circles. She could smell it on them. She could smell *everything* on them, she realized a moment later as she sniffed the air like an animal. She could smell their fears, their anger, their frustration. She could smell their lust, their hatred, their greed. None of it smelled good. None of it was good.

"We are closed," said the owner, stepping back from the counter. "Come back in the morning."

"The lights are on, the door is unlocked, and the shelves are stocked," said the second man, grinning wide as he put a badly-rolled cigarette between his tobacco-stained teeth and tried to light a match.

The owner stepped out from behind the counter and nonchalantly flipped off the light switch, plunging the store into semi-darkness. Then he shuffled over to the door and flipped the sign around, holding the door open as he smiled at the men.

"Now the lights are off and the door is about to be locked," he said pleasantly. "Good day, gentlemen.

Allah be with you in this time of trouble and chaos."

"Trouble and chaos? We love trouble and chaos! We are having a wonderful time!" said the third man, leaning over and grabbing the book of matches from the drunk second man. He lit the man's cigarette before lighting one more for himself and then tossing the burning match towards the old man.

Bis felt her arm reach out and grab the match, her fingers closing on it just right so she wouldn't burn herself. Her own quickness shocked her, and she blinked in surprise as she drew her arm back in and blew out the burning match, glaring at the two men with a ferociousness that she felt in every muscle in her body.

Oh no, she thought. Not now. This can't happen now! How do I control it?! How do I . . .

"Ya Allah!" gasped the first man, his eyes going wide as if he'd suddenly sobered the hell up. "What is she?! What . . . how . . ."

Bismeeta's vision had narrowed to a laser-focused beam, and she swore she could see her own reflection in the men's widened eyes. Except it wasn't her reflection. It wasn't the reflection of a human. It was an animal of some kind, dark and shiny like the night itself. She tried to scream as she felt her clothes rip at the seams, her body expanding, sinews tightening, muscles flexing. Muscles? When did she get muscles?!

She screamed, but the scream that emerged from

Bismeeta wasn't a scream—it was a low growl that rumbled throughout her body. Even the old man had retreated to the corner of the store and was trembling in fear, muttering every Arabic prayer he remembered. The first man had already bolted for the door, but the second was either too stupid or too drunk to run.

Instead he reached beneath his tunic and pulled out a knife, curved and long, its metal blade dull but still sharp enough to do some damage.

"Die, demon!" he shouted, swiping at her with the knife. "Cut her!" he screamed to his remaining buddy as he slashed at Bis once more.

Bis wasn't sure what happened next, but she knew no one was going to cut her. In a flash she felt her right arm move out again—except it wasn't an arm: it was a paw. Heavy and black, with claws sharper than any knife. Her head was buzzing with an energy she could barely contain, and time slowed down as she saw four blood-red marks appear on her attacker's cheek almost out of nowhere. He screamed as the blood rolled down his face, and then he dropped the knife and crashed out of the store, his buddy already five steps ahead of them, both of them howling to Allah to save them from what they clearly thought was some kind of demon.

I *am* a demon, Bis thought as she heard herself hiss and growl. She circled the store, sniffing the drops of blood, driven by pure instinct. The scent was strong, and she felt a strange urge to hunt those men, to stalk them in the night, pick them off one by one with the stealth of a cat, the precision of a trained killer. She almost did go after them, but then she heard voices coming down the street toward the store and panic set in.

"Oh, Allah, it's the military police," she muttered, surprised to hear her own voice come through. Was she talking out loud or were these her thoughts? As the panic rose, she searched frantically for her clothes, but the stolen robes were a tattered mess on the floor. Not that she was getting back into them anyway. Not like this. Not as an . . . animal!

Suddenly the lights in the store flashed bright, and Bis screamed as if she was blinded. She heard men shouting, and she hissed at them, backing away even though she knew she could kill all of them in a matter of minutes.

So kill them and run away, she thought. Do it, you beast! What are you waiting for?!

It took her a moment to realize she was actually talking to this creature—this creature who was a part of her. It struck her as insane, almost comical. But then the beast answered, and Bis almost fainted.

We are waiting for fate, whispered the animal. *And now it is here.*

Bis swooned as a dizziness washed over her so suddenly she felt herself sit down hard on her ass. She squealed in pain, and when she felt the cool tiles on her bare skin, she realized in a panic that she was human again! A human woman, naked and vulnerable!

"Come back!" she screamed, not sure who or what she was talking to. "I need you!"

He needs you, whispered that voice in her head—or was it in her body. *The bear needs you. These men will take you to him, even if they do not know it. Have some faith. Some faith in fate.*

Bismeeta backed up against the wall, pulling her legs up against her chest and hunching down to cover her nakedness. The military police at this time of lawlessness were no more trustworthy than the street thugs she'd just chased away. This was not going to end well for her. A naked woman after nightfall in a war-torn country? No, this was not a good setup.

But no man touched her. She could feel them closing in, but she also felt their fear. Finally she blinked and looked up at them, immediately recognizing the one she'd slashed across the face. He was holding his bleeding cheek and staring, muttering something in Arabic to one of the policemen, who slowly began to nod.

"There have been rumors of these creatures," the bleeding man was saying. "They change into animals. Some kind of magic. Evil."

"She does not look like an animal to me," said the policeman, frowning and pulling on his beard. "At least not the kind you described."

"Then who or what did this to me?" the bleeding man demanded, pulling his hand back from his face and showing the policeman the four perfectly aligned claw-marks.

"The old man must have a cat," said the policeman, but his expression betrayed his realization that no house cat could have done that.

"A cat the size of three men," rasped the bleeding man.

The policeman sighed, rubbing his eyes and shaking his head. "So what do you want us to do? Arrest her? We can take her in for public indecency. Or perhaps we can—"

"No," said the bleeding man, lowering his voice and glancing at the policeman. "You do not understand what we have here. She can make us rich. We will sell her!"

The policeman frowned again, his gaze moving along Bismeeta's thick thighs, her large butt, her round face before he snorted. "She is a fat whore in her thirties. We will not get much for her from the insurgents who buy women for their warriors."

The bleeding man shook his head. "No, we will not sell her to the insurgents. We will sell her to Sheikh

Murad. There are rumors he has been buying and capturing these creatures for years. He will pay well. He will pay anything we ask."

Bis felt her anger rise at the way the men were speaking about her, and although she could feel that animal clench and hiss inside her, it didn't come out. It was holding back, taking the insults, tolerating the tension. It was almost like it knew something Bis didn't, like it sensed that this was all part of a plan.

Whose plan, Bis wondered as the policeman sighed again, rubbed his beard, and then grabbed a clean white tablecloth from behind the pastry counter. He tossed it at Bis, keeping his distance and gesturing to his fellow officers to close in.

"All right," he ordered. "Take her. Let us see how much this Sheikh Murad of the desert will pay for this woman you say is some kind of animal."

4

His animal leapt to its feet as if electrocuted, and Bart growled as he blinked in the darkness of his cage. The desert sun had set hours ago, and Bart had settled down for some rest—rest like he hadn't had in years. It was strange—even though he was still trapped in bear form, the beast seemed to be relaxed, even calm. After years of being in a nonstop state of destructive anger, now that it was trapped in a magic-infused cage, it had decided to chill the hell out!

Or it had last night, at least. But now it was awake and alert again. Alert and alive with an excitement that felt like . . . like . . .

She is here, said the bear with a certainty that surprised Bart.

"Who?" he said.

Our mate. She is here. Not far. I can smell her.

Bart raised his snout and sniffed the air. He picked up the scent of several women—which was not surprising, because over the past few days Murad's men had ushered woman after woman into the bear's presence. All of them were terrified. All of them screamed for mercy, convinced they were about to be fed to a bear. But Bart had ignored them. His bear had been unmoved, simply shaking its shaggy head and retreating to its corner until Magda or Murad stopped by and ordered the woman to be replaced. It was comical, really, and once Bart figured out that his bear had enough control that it was neither going to eat the women nor try to mate with them, he'd even had some fun with it.

"Hello! I'm Bart!" he'd said to the third woman, grinning like a fool when she started to howl louder than he'd heard any animal do it. "I'm a man trapped inside a bear's body. What's your story?"

"I'm hungry," he'd whispered to the fourth girl. "They fed me a hundred rats for dinner, but it wasn't enough. May I search your hair for some lice to eat?"

To the fifth girl he'd reached out a paw in an attempt at a handshake, but the woman immediately fainted, and so Bart decided that perhaps he should stop playing around and just ignore the rest. He didn't want to actually scare anyone to death. He wasn't that kind of monster—at least he didn't think he was! Who the hell knew, though. It had been so long since he'd walked on two feet as a man.

But now he could feel the man inside him yearn to get out. And then he swore he could smell her—his mate! He breathed deep, gulping the air in along with her sweet smell like it was a drug. She smelled of sandalwood and sweetened milk, warm sugar syrup and clean perspiration. Her scent got closer as he felt his bear begin to pace its cage restlessly, and Bart began to pant as he smelled her heat, her feminine musk, the aroma of her sex.

"Oh, shit," he groaned as he felt the man in him push against the bear. In that moment he knew the bear was right. He had a mate, and she was here. There could be no doubt. After all, he'd just had twenty women paraded in front of him, and not one of them had even warranted a second sniff, despite many of them being just fine to look at. And now he was almost out of his mind with lust just from the *scent* of this new woman! He hadn't even seen the chick!

Do not call her a chick when you meet her, warned the bear like it was suddenly an expert in human romance. *She might be offended. Be polite.*

Bart snorted as he looked down at his paws, his mind twisting as he imagined them turning back into human hands, his claws disappearing, making way for fingers . . . fingers that were going to close tight on this woman's big nipples, pinching them so damned hard that she would—

Control, growled his bear. *This is a delicate situation. I will not give control back to the man if you do not show some self-control, you lust-filled animal!*

"*You* are talking about self-control?!" said Bart, swatting aimlessly at the cage, making it rattle as the bars glowed with that dark magical light that seemed to make the metal indestructible. "We spent years smashing trees, killing people, and doing God-knows-what-else thanks to your lack of control!"

I was frustrated because we were not being connected to our mate, said the bear. *Now she is here, and I am calm.*

"Oh, so now you're calm? *Calm*?! That's great news," muttered Bart. "So let me Change back while you retreat to your cave and meditate like a good bear. Go on now. The man will handle this. Good job on getting us this far, but now I'll take over."

The bear rumbled as the sounds of footsteps came through the large wooden door at the far end of the room. Bart went quiet, squinting in the darkness as his ears perked up.

"We should keep the cat Shifter in a separate room," came Murad's voice from outside the door. "Why do you want her in the same room as the bear?"

"I would like her cage to be as close as possible

to the bear's cage," came Magda's response. "If she Changes, then she will need to be held in a magic-strengthened cage or else she might break loose. And I cannot spread my magic out to so many different rooms."

Murad was silent, and Bart could hear the man breathe. "I think your magic is strong enough to handle two cages in different rooms. I think you want these two in the same room for another reason."

"And what would that be?" said Magda.

"You think she might be the bear's mate. All that talk of fated mates being drawn together by the universe through coincidences and seemingly random events. An event like this one: Us getting offered a woman who might be a Shifter out of the blue," said Murad somewhat scornfully.

"Perhaps," said Magda after a pause. "You must admit that it was unexpected how the bear made no attempt to mate with any of the women we offered it. If uniting the bear with its fated mate is the only way to Change it back to human, then this is worth a try."

"All right. Why not. But then why even have a separate cage? Just toss the woman in with the bear! If the bear Changes to a man and mates with her, then we have our answer! In fact we will have many answers!"

Magda was quiet for a bit, her breathing slow and steady. "But if they are not mates and she is indeed a Shifter, she might Change in order to protect herself from the bear. They might fight, and if they do, we have no way of stopping the fight until it is over—until one of them is dead. That is no way to build an army of Shifters, by having them kill one another, yes, Sheikh?"

Murad sighed. "All right. So we put them in adjoining cages, and if he Changes back to a man, we will unite them and let them do what animals do."

"Humans are animals too, lest you forget," said Magda quietly, almost under her breath, her voice so low that Bart wasn't sure if the old man had heard. Didn't matter, because the door was opening now, and the sweet scent of his mate floated in with the nighttime breeze, almost making the bear and man swoon like they were dancing to a silent melody.

It is her, panted the bear from inside him. *All right, you win. You will have control back. You will Change back to a man. We cannot wait. We have waited too long for our mate. Change back, and they will put her in the cage with us. You wanted to be a man again, and here we go. Here I go. Be gentle with her, Bart. Wait, what am I saying?! Take her, Bart! Take her like a beast takes its mate! Taste her nectar, smell her juices, kiss her so hard you both have bruises! Lick her between her legs, spank her buttocks, ram that Army Ranger cock of yours so deep up into her that she chokes! Get her so pregnant that she delivers bear-cubs once a month for the rest of her life! Claim her, Bart! She is ours! Claim her!*

"Shut up, you idiot," Bart whispered through clenched teeth as he tried to think, tried to put together everything he'd heard just now. Thinking wasn't his thing, but it most certainly wasn't his bear's thing, so his own mind was all he had. His mind that was rapidly weakening as four men pushed a golden cage into the room—a cage with a dark woman dressed in white sitting in the middle cross-legged and calm, her eyes closed.

Oh, shit, she's beautiful, Bart thought as he felt his mouth hang open as the cage was wheeled into the splintered moonlight streaking its way across the room. Smooth brown skin. Pretty round face. Thick red lips. Almond-shaped eyes. And those curves . . . holy fucking hell . . . are those her nipples pushing up against her robe?! Dark and round and big like saucers! Oh, shit, I wanna suck on them until they harden in my mouth! To hell with thinking! I want her! I want her *now*!

Bart could already feel the Change coming on, and he gritted his teeth and willed it back. He wasn't sure why, but he needed to keep it a secret that she was his mate. Obviously Magda and Murad weren't certain. Would the woman know? Maybe not. She might not even be a Shifter, in which case she'd be just as terrified as the others who'd been tossed into his cage! He needed time to think! What would happen if he let on that she was his mate? Murad and Magda would then put them together and let them go at it, right? But why?

Because they wanted her to get pregnant.

They wanted the offspring of their union.

That was their entire plan, wasn't it? Capture Shifters and breed them to build a new generation of Shifter warrior-slaves! Was that what Bart wanted? To be an animal in a cage, tossed together with his mate a couple of times a year so they could produce more babies for Murad's army?

We are not Changing yet, he thought firmly as he felt the bear try to give up control. I must be crazy for not taking back control when I have a chance, but I need to stay in bear form a little bit longer. Just a bit longer, all right?

The bear growled in reluctant agreement, and Bart exhaled slowly as he settled down in the cage, trying to appear as nonchalant as he had with the other women. But it was hard when they placed her cage right next to his.

And it was even harder when the woman finally opened her eyes.

Big brown eyes the size of a cat's on a moonless night.

Big brown eyes that were looking right at him . . .

. . . looking right *into* him.

5

Bismeeta saw a bear, but she knew it was a man. She could see right through the beast like it was just a costume, just window-dressing, camouflage.

He's like me, was her first thought when she looked into his eyes. Dark brown and intense, hardened and weary, but with something behind them that made her heart leap. She knew in an instant that this beast would never hurt her although he'd hurt others before and would probably hurt others in the future. She knew in an instant that this bear was hers, that she was his, that they were mates just like whatever inside her had said she was born for.

"I was born for you," she said softly, not sure where

the words were coming from, not sure whether the bear could even understand what she was saying. The room was empty now, and Bis glanced around quickly, noting the blinking video cameras mounted high up near the ceilings, at least three of them pointing down and recording everything. Did they have sound? She didn't see any microphones, and the cameras were too far away to pick up a whisper.

"I know," said the bear, making no move at all to get closer to her. It was almost like it was acting, pretending, putting on a show for the cameras. "I'm glad you know it too. Now we just need to make sure no one else figures that out. Not yet, at least."

Bis frowned, but she followed the bear's cue and stayed put in her cross-legged position, nodding just enough to let him know she understood he meant Sheikh Murad and the woman in red. She'd heard of Sheikh Murad before. She had no idea who the woman was, though. She'd seen them talking outside the door before they wheeled her cage into the room, but she'd been too far away to hear what they were saying.

One glance at the bear's fuzzy ears told Bis that this animal had heard everything. It could probably even hear her heart beat! Shit, why was her heart beating so fast? And why was she so damned hot even though there was a nice chill to the dry desert air at night?

We are in heat, came the whisper from inside her, and just then Bis took a breath and realized she was wet between her legs! *We are hot for him. He is our mate, and soon he will Change to a man and will claim you. Get ready, love. He's going to pound you with everything he's got, and it will be magnificent! We will have his babies every year and live happily ever after for the next three centuries! Now, when he takes you, be sure to get on your knees and raise your rear end high, spread your thighs as far as you can, and make sure he empties those balls deep inside you. All right, love? Oh, and don't be shocked if we start to purr, howl, and roar when we come.*

Bismeeta almost choked on her next breath as she listened to the animal speak in full sentences inside her damned head like it was a fairy godmother! A dirty, filthy, horny fairy godmother with a clear lack of understanding of what was happening here!

"What's happening here?" she finally whispered, her voice so low she knew that only the bear would be able to hear. "Do you know?"

The bear didn't speak. It just blinked slowly, both eyes at once. Bis felt a strange chill rush through her—a sense of excitement, even security, like this massive bear was going to protect her, save her, figure this out and make everything all right!

"Don't Change," muttered the bear under its breath.

"What?" said Bis. "Don't change what?"

"Yourself," said the bear. "Stay human, and perhaps they will let you go."

Bis blinked. She could feel her animal hiss from

inside her, like the very thought of being separated from this bear was a non-starter.

"Are you a cat Shifter?" said the bear when she didn't reply.

Bis shuddered in surprise. He knew! How did he know?! "You mean like a Siamese cat?" she said, blinking and holding back a smile. Of course he knew! "I don't know what I am, actually. I've always been out of my senses when it happened, and I don't think I ever looked in a mirror."

The bear snorted softly, sniffing with its snout and then grunting. "Yes, you are a cat. But not that kind of cat. A big cat."

Bis frowned as she looked down at herself, sucking in her cheeks and her belly at the same time until she almost fainted from the lack of oxygen. "A *big* cat? As in a *fat* cat? That is a bit rude and presumptuous, don't you think?"

The bear's eyes moved, and Bis could tell it was the man inside looking at her. She pulled her robe tighter, but she felt her animal push at her from the inside, like it was restless, impatient. It took her a moment to realize she'd just thought of that creature inside her as "her animal," and then it struck her as shameful that she hadn't even had the courage to figure out what it was! A cat? Big cat?

"I mean big cat like a lion, leopard, panther. Maybe a cougar," said the bear hurriedly. "I didn't mean fat. You aren't . . . I mean, you're not . . . never mind."

Bis smiled as she felt herself relax a bit—which was strange, because she was locked in a cage and talking to a bear so large it could squash ten of her with just its left hind paw.

"So you didn't mean fat, but yet you won't say I'm *not* fat. Also, you shouldn't call a woman over thirty a cougar."

The bear grinned, showing long, savage teeth that once again didn't scare Bis in the least. She didn't even think she could see the bear. She only saw what was inside—the man himself. What did he look like, she wondered. Was she going to see him in the flesh soon? Was she going to . . . oh, God, what was she thinking?!

Yes, you are going to do exactly that with him, whispered her "big cat" from where it was crouching in the back of her consciousness like it was assessing the situation, its impatience growing. *Now can we get a move on, please? That is enough chatter. He wants you. You want him. What more is there to talk about?*

"There's a lot to talk about," Bis said firmly, ignoring the fact that she sounded crazy for talking to herself. Then she glanced at the bear and realized that no, she didn't sound crazy at all—not around him. Not around her . . . mate?

"Keep your voice low," said the bear softly. "I don't know for sure, but I assume they're watching and listening."

"Watching, yes," Bis said, glancing up at the cameras. "But I don't know about listening."

"Why would they *not* be listening?" said the bear. "If they put cameras in here, then why not microphones?"

Bis glanced around the cavernous room. The floor was rough sandstone, and there were open balconies at the far sides of the space. She could see the stars from her cage, and she knew they were still in the desert. Somewhere in the lawless land between Syria and Iraq, where borders were meaningless, militia roamed the sands, and it was like the Wild West of old America—a free for all, where men took what they wanted. That was what she'd heard about Murad, who'd simply been a wealthy man who'd seized land and declared himself Sheikh of all he surveyed!

"I don't know why they wouldn't be listening," said Bis. "Perhaps they don't believe that you can talk when in bear form."

The bear grunted. "Maybe. Though I didn't think Adam's father would be that ignorant about Shifters."

"Sheikh Murad, you mean?"

The bear snorted. "He's not a Sheikh! Not a real one, at least. That would mean Adam is royalty, and trust me, that arrogant dragon would have made it known if he was of royal blood."

Bis bolted upright, her eyes going wide at the mention of a dragon. "Dragon? You know the dragon?"

"Adam Drake? Hell yeah, I know him! He was my commanding officer when we were put together on that disaster of a Black Ops mission." The bear shook his shaggy head, and Bis could sense the emotion in the beast. "What was Benson thinking?! We weren't ready for that. None of us were!"

"What happened?" she said softly. Even though she had a million other questions about everything the bear had just said—Murad, the dragon, Adam Drake, John Benson—she somehow thought this was the most important one. It was the most important part of the bear's story, and she wanted to hear that part first. His part first.

"I lost control of the animal," he said stoically even though a deep rumble emerged from the body of the bear. "We were sent in to extract hostages. CIA informants who'd been deeply embedded in a terrorist sleeper cell based in South America. It was a delicate operation. Too delicate for a blunt instrument like me."

Bis sighed as she listened to this hulk of a bear speak with a depth of feeling that should seem comical but was almost heartbreaking. She could feel his pain like it was hers. How could that be? She didn't even know him! She still hadn't even seen what he looked like—at least not as a man.

"What's your name?" she asked, realizing that they were already getting deep into conversation but they didn't even know each other's names. "I'm Bismeeta. Bis for short."

"Bis," said the bear. "I like that. I'm Bart. Bartholomew for long. And if you ever call me that, I'll rip you to shreds."

"Um, OK," said Bis, her eyes going wide as she glanced at the bear's gigantic black claws. "I'll try to keep that in mind. Note to self: Do not call the bear by his full name or he will murder you. Got it."

Bart chuckled, the sound reverberating through Bis's body, making her tingle and want to laugh. But then she remembered that they were being watched, and she just kept a straight face.

"You are Arab," said Bart after a while.

"Yes. And you're American?"

"Damn straight. Red, white, and blue, baby."

Bis smiled. "And you're a soldier?"

"Yes, ma'am. At least I was. You?"

"Not a soldier," said Bis with a quick shake of the head. "I'm a teacher."

"Huh. OK. I can see that, I guess. What do you teach?"

"English," said Bis.

"Where?" said the bear.

"Damascus."

"Syria? I didn't think there were any school buildings left standing after the Russians, Americans, Saudis, and Iranians got done with their bombing."

Bis let out a regretful laugh. "I know you're joking, but you're sort of right. My school building almost got blown away a few months ago. Three bombs missed us by a few hundred feet." She laughed again. "Though the kids like the new landscaping effect the craters give the schoolyard."

The bear grunted. "Kids. Innocent. Clueless. A pain in the ass."

Bis felt her cat clench inside her, hissing as it twirled its invisible tail, swiped its ethereal paws at the bear. "You don't like kids?" she said, folding her arms under her breasts, fighting back the image of little bear-human-cat babies suckling at her nipples as she oozed fresh milk.

He lies, her animal rasped from inside her. *Take off your robe and he will be crying for mama as he breaks through his cage and puts his seed into you.*

"OK, that's just weird and disgusting," muttered Bis, turning her head sideways as she reprimanded her animal. "Now shut up. I'll handle this, all right?"

"It's strange, isn't it?" said Bart just then.

"What's strange?"

"Having that animal inside you, whispering to you like it's a living, breathing creature."

Bis blinked, her breath catching sharply. "Isn't it a living, breathing creature?"

"Yes and no. It's real and alive. But it's also just a part of you. It *is* you."

Bis snorted. "Um, I don't think so. I'm not a violent person, and whatever's inside me most certainly is."

"Humans are more violent than all the animals

put together. No species inflicts more pain and suffering on its own kind than we do. Our animals use violence for protection, defending their young, and finding food. Their motives are pure and simple. Human motives, however . . . they are . . ."

". . . complicated," said Bis, finishing his sentence and nodding. "Tell me about it."

"No," said the bear. "I want you to tell me things. It's been so long since I've heard a human voice. A woman's voice. It reminds me that I'm still a man trapped inside this furry costume."

"Trapped? Why do you say that? Can't you Change back and forth at will?"

The bear grunted, its dark eyes flashing as if the man inside yearned to break free but was holding himself back for some reason. "Can *you* Change back and forth at will?"

Bis shrugged. Then she shook her head. "I didn't know I could Change at all until a few months ago. After I saw the dragon."

Bart's eyes flicked wide open. "Wait, you saw Adam Drake?"

"I think so. I saw a dragon. It didn't tell me its name. It was too busy killing, burning, and feeding."

The bear raised its head and grinned, its eyes flashing with energy. "Sounds like Adam's dragon. What color were its eyes?"

"One green, one gold," said Bis.

"Shit, that's Adam! Where did you see him? What did he say?"

Bis shrugged as she thought back to that chaotic day. "I don't know where, exactly. Somewhere in Athraak province. I was in a truck with a group of women who'd been kidnapped as war-brides and sex-slaves. The dragon swooped in out of nowhere, breathing fire and . . . and *eating* people!"

The bear shrugged. "Man's gotta eat," he said nonchalantly. "Bad guys taste as good as anyone else, so might as well eat the assholes of the human race."

"Ew," said Bis even though she could feel her cat growl in agreement, reminding her that it was not just horny but also hungry. "But all right. Anyway, he killed the drivers of our truck, and then . . ." She paused as she thought back to what the dragon had said to the women.

"And then what? Come on, Bis. Don't leave me hangin'! Damn, I wish I was back out there with the dragon, raiding, rampaging, killing the assholes of the world!"

Bis laughed as she saw the soldier in him come to life. In that moment she knew he was good, no matter what he'd done, no matter what mistakes he'd made.

"Well," she said, laughing as she remembered what that dragon had said, "it sounds weird now that I think back. But the dragon told all of us to go home, to go to our lovers and mates, to . . . to make *babies*!"

Bart roared with laughter, the massive body of his bear shaking like jelly. He rolled onto his back, his legs pawing at the sky as he laughed and rolled around his cage. Bis was laughing too, and although she knew they were being watched, she didn't give a damn.

"Babies? *Babies*?! God-damn, Adam! You've lost it, brother! Shit, man! What happened to us? I'm in a cage, and you're roaming the desert lecturing people about having babies?!"

Bis frowned, forcing the smile off her face as she watched the killer beast roll around on its back like an oversized bear-cub. "What's wrong with having babies?"

The bear finally stopped laughing and rolled over to face her. "You just don't know Adam," he said. "Dragons are loners. They fly free and unattached. In a million years I could never imagine Adam Drake having goddamn dragon babies!"

Bis was silent for a moment, her gaze taking in the sight of the bear, her imagination once again forming a picture of the man inside the beast. "What about bears?" she asked softly. "Are they loners too?"

"I am," said Bart quickly—far too quickly, Bis thought.

"Just because you've been alone for years doesn't mean you're a loner," said Bis quietly, thinking back to how long she'd been alone, without a man. She'd been on dates when she was studying in England, but they'd never progressed beyond a date or two, a kiss or two. It wasn't that she was too prudish to sleep with a man before they were married or something. She just hadn't felt it with anyone she'd ever met. Never. Not until now. Not until him. And still she didn't even know what he looked like! It was unreal. Surreal. Not real. A fairy-tale, but twisted around, topsy-turvy. Like *Beauty and the Beast* on steroids. Or LSD. "Don't you have any family? Parents? Siblings?"

The bear growled. "My parents hated me. They hated what I was. They spent their lives trying to save me from the Shifter disease—at least that's what they called it. I called it child abuse."

Bis narrowed her eyes, wondering if he was serious. "Your parents were not Shifters?" Is that what I am, she wondered at the same time—a Shifter? The carrier of a disease? What about *my* parents?! Did they know? Did they do this to me? Were they the same as I am?

"They were bears," said Bart. "They worked for the US Department of Defense as scientists. Their pet project was developing a drug to make their kids 'normal'—whatever the hell that meant."

Bis giggled. "*Pet* project? That is a good one."

"A good what?" said the bear. "Oh, I see," he snorted after a moment. He snickered, his massive body shaking in the moonlight as Bis watched.

A wave of the most delightful warmth passed

through Bis as she relaxed and lay down on her side, her face turned toward the bear. I'm talking to a bear, she told herself. A bear who speaks like a man. I'm talking to him, and I'm . . . I'm . . . falling in . . . no! No way! Impossible! I don't even know what he looks like! I can't be falling in love with a man I've never even seen!

You are not falling in love with him, whispered her animal. *You are already in love with him. That is what fate means, you ignorant human.*

"I'm sure your parents meant well," she said quickly, not wanting to engage with her restless animal right now. She wanted to engage with Bart. It felt good. It felt right. It felt—

Engage with him, said her animal, *and soon you'll be engaged!*

Bis rolled her eyes, holding back the comment that her cat's jokes were lame. She focused on the bear once again, and seeing that he clearly didn't want to talk about his parents, that even mentioning them made him angry, she moved on.

"Siblings?" she said. "Brothers? Sisters?"

The bear sighed. "I had a sister. She was still a baby when I left for the Army. I haven't seen her since."

Bart paused as he said the last sentence, his furry brow crinkling up as if in confusion, like he wasn't sure that he was speaking the truth.

"What is it?" Bis asked. "What did you just think of?"

The bear blinked and grunted. "Nothing. I don't know. Probably nothing. Just a memory of the day I got captured. I coulda sworn I saw another bear, but the memory isn't clear. I was out of my mind. Wasn't thinking straight. Certainly wasn't seeing straight."

Bis nodded. "Bears aren't known for having great eyesight," she said.

"I didn't realize you also taught zoology, biology, and optometry," retorted the bear.

Big giggled. "And I didn't realize you knew such big words, Bart the Bear."

Bart growled with stifled laughter. "All right, Teacher. No, my bear doesn't have great eyesight. The dragon was the one in our crew who could see ten miles ahead, through fog and rain. I was the muscle. I broke things, and I did it damned well."

"I'm sure you did," Bis said, smiling as she pictured the man inside the beast—a man rippling with muscles, thighs thick as tree-trunks, a back broader than her dining table, arms sinewy and heavy, fists the size of sledgehammers.

Don't worry, love. He won't break you, but he will break you in, purred her horny cat. *And you know you want him to break you in. Hold you down and pound you. Break you in like a naughty teacher.*

"OK, naughty teacher is not a thing," Bis muttered, turning her head away from Bart and whispering to her animal even though she knew she sounded insane. But then she realized that no, given present company, this was perfectly normal!

"What's your animal saying?" Bart asked.

"Nothing. Just babbling nonsense."

The bear's nostrils moved as it sniffed the air. "It is in heat," Bart whispered. "It wants us to mate. But we can't. Not now."

"No, of course not," Bis said hurriedly, pressing her thighs together as she lay on her side facing the bear. Could he . . . could he *smell* her heat?! Ohmygod, how sick was that! How gross, disgusting, twisted . . . and . . . and *erotic*!

Bis felt the wetness between her legs as her mind once again was ambushed by images of the man emerging from the bear, naked and hard, muscled like a Greek god, his eyes focused on her, his need focused on her, everything focused on her. She imagined him pulling apart the bars to her cage, pulling her legs apart, jamming his stubbled face between her thighs and licking her until she spread wide for him. And then . . .

"Of course we can't," she said again, forcing her eyes open wide as she felt the arousal make her sick with need. She took deep, gulping breaths, swallowing hard and staring into Bart's eyes like she knew

him. "Um, why not? I mean, I know we're not going to, of course. We can't, since we're in separate
cages—and, of course, you're a bear. Then there are
these video cameras focused on us, so of course we
can't. I'm just asking, though. Not that we would,
ever. Never, I mean."

Bart laughed as Bis felt herself go bright red under her brown skin. She was babbling like a school-
girl, she knew. Her animal's need was driving her insane, making her stupid with lust, tongue-tied with
arousal. God, she was making a fool of herself, wasn't
she? Well, that was one way to ensure this wasn't
happening!

He will Change for you, whispered her cat. *He is close.
His bear wants to retreat and let the man take over, let
the man take his mate, take you! Keep pushing!*

But Bis frowned as she thought back to what Bart
had whispered to her early on, when they'd first been
put next to each other. He'd said "Don't Change" to
her, and she could feel that he was holding back his
own Change. He wanted them to stay as they were:
She in human form; he as a bear. He had a plan.

"They want to breed us," said the bear, his voice
straining as if he was holding back his rage. "Breed
us like dumb beasts, like freaks. But they don't know
for sure that you're a Shifter. And they don't know for
sure that you're my mate." He went quiet, his savage
eyes softening in a way that almost melted Bis into

the sandstone floor. "Only we know for sure right now. And it needs to stay that way. It's our only shot at getting you out of here."

"But I don't want to get out," Bis said, sidling up to the edge of her cage and reaching across to him. But their cages were too far apart, and her outstretched arm just stayed there, fingers extended, reaching for something she couldn't have—not yet. "I was led here. Led to you."

"I know," he said, rolling his massive body to the edge of his own cage and trying to reach for her hand. But the bear's paws were too damned big to fit through the bars, and he growled as he clawed at the metal, which glimmered with the dark light of the witch's magic. "Our animals drew us together. They are primal forces within us, oblivious to the complications of human affairs. But we need to balance those physical needs with the greater needs of the situation." He paused again, taking a long breath as he rolled onto his back and stared up at the ceiling. "You need to get out of here. Find Adam Drake. Find the dragon."

6

"They are dragons!" shouted Adam, holding up his twin babies like trophies as they squealed in delight. "I know it!"

Ash giggled as she stared up at the proud father. It had been three days since she'd delivered the twins, the birth coming naturally, smoothly, like it was meant to be—like it was all meant to be. They'd spent the past few months in Adam's castle in the middle of the Caspian Sea, doing nothing but being together—together in every way, shape, and form possible. Together in every position too, Ash reminded herself as she felt her bear whisper that now that she'd delivered the twins, she was ready to get knocked up again!

"Um, they're human babies, Adam," she told him patiently as she watched him run around the room with his children in his arms. "They might not even be Shifters, you know."

"They are dragons," said Adam firmly, cradling them and looking down at her with those gold-and-green eyes. He took a breath, his gaze resting on her milk-laden breasts that felt so heavy that Ash swore she was getting back pain from the added weight. "And the next set will be bears. And on and on till eternity. Bears, dragons, and everything in between."

Ash laughed as her husband got into the sprawling king-sized bed with her, placing her newborns on her breasts. He pulled her robe aside, making her gasp as her breasts popped out, nipples big and red. Adam groaned as he pinched each nipple hard with his strong fingers, but Ash pushed his hands away so her children could feed.

"These aren't for you right now," she scolded as her children started to suckle and Adam sighed and lay back down beside her. "But maybe tonight when the children are asleep."

"The children will be asleep in a few minutes, the way they are drinking," growled Adam, reaching for the bottom of her robe until she clamped her thighs closed tight and pulled his hands away. "All right. All right. I will wait until tonight. But you're going to pay the price for making me wait, woman."

Ash shuddered as she pictured what was in store for her that night. Adam had been relatively gentle with her pregnant body, and she knew that there were some pent-up needs in her man that would have to be met. She could barely wait to "pay the price" for making him wait!

But as they lay together, the new Shifter family, the only sound in the room the gentle suckling of two babies mixed in with the roar of the waves of the blue Caspian Sea that surrounded their island fortress, Ash knew that soon enough they'd have to turn their attention to the bigger picture—the bigger family issues that needed to be resolved: Ash's brother Bart; Adam's father Murad.

Adam had refused to even discuss looking for Bart and Murad while she was pregnant with his children. The dragon's protective instincts were too strong to entertain any discussion of putting his wife and children at even the smallest risk while she was vulnerable and with child. But she knew that Adam the man was thinking about it in the background just like she was. He'd said Bart was a soldier, a military-man, a Shifter as strong as any he'd ever seen. He would survive until Adam and Ash came for him. He would survive, because there was another person coming for him too: His mate, whoever she was.

7

She came for you, and now you want to send her away? whispered the bear, its rage bubbling up as Bart fought back the need to Change and take his mate. *I thought the man was the brains of this operation, but clearly you are as dumb as any bear. Change now! Take your mate! And everything will work out! Have some faith, you dumbass!*

"If I Change, they will know she is my mate, and then neither of us will ever see the light of day," Bart said out loud, talking to both Bis and his bear.

Who cares, said the bear. *What were we doing in the light of day, anyway? Roaming, rampaging, raging? Stay here and we will have our mate! Always and forever! That is all we need!*

"It isn't and you damned well know it," growled Bart, snapping his teeth as if he wanted to fight his bear. "We need to roam free, to rampage once in a while, to unleash some rage on the wicked! We need it all to be complete. We need it all, and we will have it all!"

"What's your bear saying?" Bis asked from across the floor, and Bart blinked as he looked into her big brown eyes, studied her pretty round face, tried not fixate on her gorgeous curves beneath that loose white robe. But damn, he could see her nipples through the sheer cloth, big and dark, like magnets drawing him in! Had Murad and that witch purposely dressed her like this to tempt him to Change back to a man and take her? He had to resist! He had to hold back that primal, raw need to mate, to reproduce, to damned well *fuck*!

He growled again, every muscle in his body tightening as he looked into her eyes. "It's saying that maybe we can have a great life just living in a cage together, mating and producing children every year. And then some bullshit about how I should just claim you and trust that everything will be all right, that the universe will make sure it all works out. Bunch of sentimental crap. Didn't know my bear was such a pussy."

Bart felt his claws extend as the bear took offense at the insult, and he grinned. Good. Let the bear remember that it was a ball of muscled rage, three tons of fury in fur, that sex and violence were the twin engines that drove the beast, whether it realized it or not. There was no place for reason in the bear's mind. That was the realm of the man.

"That is an option, you know," said Bis, her face turning slightly red as she spoke. "What are the chances they let me leave here alive anyway? Even if they decide that I'm not a Shifter and not your mate, you believe they'll just let me walk away? I already know too much, don't I?"

Bart frowned as a chill ran through him. Shit, she was right, wasn't she? He was a goddamn moron! No wonder his job in the crew was mostly to break things!

"So you want to live in a zoo the rest of your life?" he snapped, not sure if he was angry at her or himself. "Give up our children to some madman who's trying to build an army of Shifters to do . . . shit, I don't even know *what* he wants to do!"

"Exactly! We don't know what he wants to do. And we need to find out, don't we?" said Bis, her face lighting up with excitement as if she was planning it all as she spoke. Damn, she was smart, wasn't she? Hell, their kids would have her brains and his brawn—what a combination! They'd be unstoppable! They'd be perfect!

Purrfect, whispered his bear as it chuckled. *Bears and cats! Kittens and cubs! Furballs with fangs! Killers with claws! Do it! Do it! Do it!*

"All right, Miss Bis," said Bart, grinning as he felt both the man and the bear in him begin to understand this smart-as-hell teacher's crazy-as-hell plan. "What do you suggest?"

"You know what I'm suggesting," said Bis, glancing at the cameras and then back into his eyes. He could see she was embarrassed at what she was thinking, but at the same time there was an openness in her, a sense of adventure, a level of faith in what they were to each other that drove straight into his heart. She believed, he could tell. She believed in him, in them, in their destiny. She was strength and beauty all rolled up in one, and in that moment Bart knew he would follow her to the ends of the Earth, protect her with his life and his death, love her until the heavens dropped down from the sky and squashed all of them like bugs.

Nice metaphor, whispered the bear. *You should write a book when this is over.*

"Shut up, wise-guy," muttered Bart, blinking as he felt his paws tighten, the claws drawing back like they were shrinking, like the Change was coming. "Let me think."

But there wasn't going to be time to think, Bart realized as he felt his eyesight get more focused, sensed his snout begin to morph back to the strong hook of his human nose, saw his paws begin to turn back into hands and feet. He wasn't going to be able to stop this any longer. He was Changing back to a man. And the man was going to take his woman.

"You're saying you want us to join Murad and the witch—or at least to pretend that we are," he gasped as the pain of the Change began to take over. It had been so long since he'd experienced being in human form that it was like a rebirth, like he was crawling out of a cocoon, reaching for the light from what had seemed like years of darkness. "You want us to . . . to go undercover? Pretend like we're going along with their plan? Destroy them from the inside?" He snorted as he felt his chest tighten into the rock-hard pectorals of Bart Brown, Army Ranger, Special Forces, Black Ops, and everything in between. "They'll never believe us!"

Bis shook her head, her eyes moving along his body as his human broke through. "Not at first. We'll have to play the long game. Convince them over time."

Bart nodded as he understood what she was saying. Make them believe that they'd been unable to stop themselves from mating, that they were fated mates and they wanted to be together no matter how, that they were willing to do anything so long as they could be together. They were surrendering, he realized. Or pretending to surrender. He wasn't sure, actually. Was she sure?

No, she isn't sure either, he realized. She's being

pushed by the animal in her just like I am. This could be the biggest mistake of our lives. We might never be able to convince Murad and Magda that we actually want to join them. We might simply be giving into our lust and dooming ourselves to become animals in a madman's zoo, beasts kept in a cage to be bred, fed, and finally put down when we're no longer of use.

But what's the other option, Bart thought as he leaned back and roared, feeling his neck strain as it tightened and then relaxed as he took in deep, gulping breaths through his human nose. She's right. They'd never let her go anyway. The only way is forward. Deeper into the pit. Except this time you aren't alone. You've got a partner. A mate. Someone who complements you, matches you at every level.

Bart heard her gasp, and when he looked down at himself he saw that he was a man again. The Change was complete, and there he was, naked and glistening with sweat from the effort of the transformation, every muscle on his hard body twitching as he took deep breaths and soaked in the oxygen. In the distance he could hear the doors of the room opening, and he knew this train had left the station. There was no turning back.

He turned on his side and looked into Bis's eyes. Her hand was still stretched out through the bars of her cage, and Bart smiled when he realized that he could reach his own arm through now. He did it, and a bolt of electricity ripped through him as their fingertips touched and he felt her heat, felt her passion, felt her need.

Felt her love.

"I knew it!" came Magda's voice from the edge of the room. "They are mates! Put her into his cage immediately, then clear the room. Oh, and please turn off the cameras. Trust me, no one wants to see what these two freaks do next."

8

Bart growled as Murad's men roughly pushed Bis-meeta into his cage and then slammed the bars shut once again. He glared at them, his naked body hard and rippling with tensed-up muscles. He stood at the back of the cage, gripping the bars behind him just to keep from leaping at those men who dared to even *touch* his mate, let alone shove her around like that! For a moment he almost let his bear come forth again, and it took everything in him to hold back the Change!

"I should have called the bear back," he rasped, his fists clenched as he watched the men leave the room at Magda's command. "And you should have Changed to your animal when they had you between cages.

We could have killed them all in a few seconds. Poof. Done. Game over."

"The witch's magic might have stopped us. Besides, killing these guards would have been pointless. Murad wasn't in the room," Bis said, blinking as she stared into his eyes like she was trying desperately not to gaze down along his nakedness . . . the nakedness of a man, not a bear. A man in heat. A man in need. A man in . . . love?

Love isn't a thing in the animal world, Bart told himself as he thought back to when he'd first heard about fated mates. It had been a conversation he'd overheard his parents having one evening when he was a kid of nine or ten. His mother had been pregnant with his baby sister at the time, and she'd been giving herself the same injections that Bart had been getting every week: Shots of some experimental drug to make them "normal" humans, to "cure" the Shifter mutation. That didn't turn out so well, did it, Mama and Papa bear?

He tried to remember what his parents had been saying about fated mates, but his memory was spotty and faded. He remembered that it was more an argument than a conversation, and it had resulted in his father Changing into his bear and crashing out of their house. Papa-bear had rampaged through the woods all night while Mama had stayed home, shooting herself up with those drugs. That was the last time he'd seen either of his parents Change. It was the last time he'd heard either of them say the words "fated mates."

"Sure," he said to his fated mate, smiling when he realized he was a man and she was a woman and they were standing a few feet from each other, looking into one another's eyes. "Murad wasn't in the room, so killing everyone else wouldn't have done shit for us. But that's not the reason we didn't Change to our animals and start killing people. It was because our animals had something else on their minds. Not violence but sex. Something that can only be done by the humans in us. The man and the woman. You and me."

Bis giggled, her pretty round face turning dark as she blushed beneath her gorgeous brown skin. Damn, she was pretty. Was she really his?

Yes, you dumb piece of muscle, roared his bear from somewhere inside. *She is yours! Now stop thinking and just take her! Claim her! Do you even remember how to use that firehose of a cock, you useless piece of human garbage?! Her cat is going wild with heat, and she will pounce on you if you don't take control of the situation like a man, you overgrown oaf!*

"Can we tone down the insults, please," Bart said to his bear, his eyes focused on Bis. He could see the cat in her eyes, feel its energy in how she was standing before him, sense its heat in her feminine scent. But it wasn't going to pounce on him. This woman was smart, strong, and adventurous, but she was still a conservative woman in many ways, Bart could tell. She wanted him, but she would wait for him to make the first move. She would dance with him all night, match his every move, but she needed him to lead her onto the dancefloor.

Slowly Bart circled her, breathing deep of her scent as he felt his arousal grow. It felt strange to know that they were in a cage together, put together like animals in a zoo while their keepers waited for them to mate. It felt sick in a way, reminding him of what he'd heard his parents argue about when he was a child, that Shifters were freaks of nature, unnatural and unholy, victims of a disease that could and should be cured.

"So many scars," came her voice, and Bart realized that she was taking in every inch of his body with her big brown eyes. She touched his chest, her eyes going wide as she circled two round scars that were mostly faded. "Are those from . . . bullets? How are you still alive?"

Bart shrugged. "It's not that easy to kill a Shifter, Bis. We heal fast and we heal well. Bullets feel like pinpricks to me. A mere annoyance. Dragons can withstand bombs, rockets, and probably a goddamn nuclear explosion. And yeah," he said, looking down into her eyes, his hand gently touching her hair, making her shudder, "you cat-Shifters are usually faster than any bullet I've seen!"

Bis snorted and looked away. "Me? Fast? I do not think so. Fast food, maybe."

Bart laughed, tilting his head back and letting himself roar with delight. Damn, it felt good to be a man again! Yeah, good to be a man, standing next to a woman. His woman.

He looked down into her eyes, touching her hair again as she looked up at him and blinked. He could feel his bear push him onward, but he wanted to take his time, slow it down, savor this moment, savor this woman. He was naked before her, nothing separating their bodies but the thin layer of her loose white robe. He knew he was hard, but he also felt in control of himself and his animal in a way he didn't think was possible. The feeling was sublime, and he almost broke down into tears when he realized that after a lifetime of struggling to gain control of his animal, suddenly it had come to him. Come to him because *she'd* come to him!

"What is it?" she asked softly. "Why are you looking at me like that?"

"You saved me," he whispered, choking back the emotion that threatened to overwhelm him.

Bis blinked and looked around. "Um, I believe we are still in a cage, trapped in a madman's castle."

"That's not what I mean. I mean you brought a balance to me just by stepping into my life. Bis, my whole damned life has been a violent struggle between man and beast, Bart and the bear, a fight for control, for balance, for . . . for *peace*! And now, suddenly, just like that, I feel in control! I feel balanced! I feel complete! You completed me, Bis! You're the missing piece!"

"I think *you're* missing a piece," she whispered, smiling with her eyes as she reached up and touched his thick hair, tapping the side of his head gently. "We're in a cage and you're talking about finding peace and balance?"

"I was in a cage even when I roamed free in the jungle," Bart growled, his hand tightening around the back of her neck. He could feel the energy surge through him—passion, arousal, need—all of that, yes. But there was also something else in what he felt when he looked into his mate's eyes: Protectiveness, possessiveness, the need to start a family with her, the need to *protect* that family with everything he had.

The thoughts roared through his mind as images of her pregnant with his cubs came through clear as day. He could see the two of them raising their family, cubs and kittens and everything in between. But along with the joy of that vision came an underlying sense of dread, a feeling of dark selfishness, the realization that once he took Bis as his mate, claimed her, put his seed in her, then she and their children would be the highest priority in his life. Both the bear and the man would live to protect and preserve their family. The feeling was so raw and deep that Bart almost choked again.

"Bis," he muttered, his fingers rubbing the back of her neck. She'd gone quiet, and he could feel her arousal as she gently purred under his touch. "Bis, I want you. I want you so bad. But . . . but . . ."

"But not like this," she whispered, nodding as she completed his sentence even though he wasn't sure how it would have ended if he'd kept talking. "I know. We need to keep our heads. Figure out how to play this."

Bart felt his bear rumble and roil inside him like it was losing patience with the man. It wanted its mate, and it didn't give a shit about the big picture. It didn't care about strategy or tactics, grand plans and elaborate schemes. It wanted its mate. It wanted its fate. It wanted . . . children.

Children.

"Leverage," said Bart, blinking as it suddenly came to him in a flash. "Bis, what's the leverage we have in this negotiation?"

Bis snorted, looking around them pointedly and then back into his eyes. "We're in a cage that even your bear's strength cannot break. I do not think we have much leverage. We are prisoners, and this is hardly a negotiation."

Bart shook his head. "John Benson used to say that it's always a negotiation, no matter what the situation. If you're still alive, it means you have something of value that the enemy wants, which means you have leverage. What do they want from us, Bis?"

Bis took a breath, her brown eyes narrowing as she thought. Then she blinked, those pretty eyes going wide with the panic of realization. "They want us to mate."

"Right. And why do they want us to mate? Because they're making a Shifter porn video for their YouTube channel? Or because they want the outcome, the result of our coupling, the offspring of our union?"

"They want our children," whispered Bis, and Bart could see the cat in her eyes hiss as it turned inside his woman. God, the animal in her gave her this electric energy that drove him wild, and he had to struggle to stop himself from putting his big human paws all over her, push her face down and take her like the beast inside him wanted. "I'll kill them," she muttered, stepping back and starting to pace. "I'll kill them. I swear it. I feel it. I know it."

"And *they* know it," said Bart triumphantly as he thought back to all those conversations he'd overheard his parents having—conversations about Shifters, about those primal needs to mate, about how protecting their children was an all-consuming drive, the most powerful force in the universe after the need to actually create those children. "They know that if they take our children, we'll do anything to keep them safe. So let's use that. Use it as a bargaining tool to do what you suggested."

"What I suggested . . ." Bis said, still pacing as if the thought of having children and giving them up was still driving her wild. "You mean the suggestion about joining Murad and Magda? Convincing them that we're willing to help them do whatever they're planning? Conquest, genocide, whatever the hell they're thinking they can do with an army of Shifters?"

"Yes. You were right—they wouldn't believe us if we just shrugged and said hey, we're on board with your crazy villainous plan. But what we *can* do is convince them that we'll do anything and everything for our children, to protect them, to be with them. And that's the truth, Bis. That's what comes from the animals inside us. Once we have kids, the protective instincts will be so powerful that right and wrong, good and evil, justice and injustice . . . none of it will matter to our animals, to us. It's the only way to convince Magda and Murad that we might actually be allies in their war, assets to their plan."

Bis let out a long, trembling breath and nodded slowly. "Because it might actually be true. We actually might become allies, willing to do anything to protect our family unit. I can feel my animal agreeing, hear it purr in approval. It wants its kittens and your cubs, and it's willing to make any compromise to get it."

Bart watched as Bis paced around the cage, her white gown flowing back, the front of it tight against her heavy breasts, her round belly, her thick thighs. He could feel himself erect like he'd never been, rock-hard and ready to take her. But he also felt in control, and he almost cried with joy as he felt the balance of power inside him. His bear was submitting to the human—for now, at least.

For now, because it understood that soon it would get what it wanted. Everything it wanted. No matter what price they had to pay.

9

Bis tried not to stare at the naked soldier at the far end of her cage, but it was hard not to look. He was built like a firetruck, tall and broad like a building, arms thicker than her thighs, high cheekbones and a massive square jaw, a chest like a barrel, abs ribbed like a washboard. And he was hers. All hers.

So long as they could pull this off.

They'd been sitting in silence for what seemed like an hour. The cameras were indeed off, and even though Bart had shouted for their captors to come in, that he wanted to talk, no one had entered the room. It was like a game of chicken, like Magda and Murad were waiting to see how long Bis and Bart could keep themselves apart, resist the need to mate.

Of course, Bis and Bart couldn't touch one another until they started the negotiation. Somehow Bis knew that the first time they mated, she'd take his seed, get pregnant, and then everything would change. Murad and Magda would know that they were just animals at heart, that they would mate year after year in captivity, producing a litter of kittens or a brood of cubs like clockwork from their golden cage. Why would the witch and the Sheikh negotiate when they were getting what they wanted anyway? No, Bis had to keep her mind on the big picture, and not her mate's big . . . oh, God, stop thinking about that!

Her breath caught as she felt her cat hiss and claw, once more pushing her to go to him, to let him take her. Bis felt her resolve waver, and a chill went through her when she realized this was going to be hard, that there was a chance she and Bart would lose this negotiation even if they won it, that there was a very real possibility that they *would* in fact do anything to be together, including lie, cheat, steal, and kill!

"Maybe they can't hear us," Bis said after a while of both of them yelling for someone to come into the room. "Maybe they're all too disgusted by the thought of what's going on in here. Maybe they won't be back for days!"

Bart's big chest moved as he took a breath, his gaze lingering on her bosom as his cock moved. He'd been hard as a post all this while, and several times Bis had seen him clench his fists and mutter under his breath like he was talking to his animal, ordering it to retreat.

"I won't last for days," Bart muttered, shaking his head and closing his eyes. The veins on his neck were bulging with the strain from controlling himself, his animal, his need. "I'm very close to just saying to hell with it and taking you now. In fact maybe I will. Yes, I will."

His brown eyes narrowed to a laser focus, and Bis felt her breath catch as she saw her mate slowly get to his feet. Her own wetness had been flowing steadily all this while, and her gown had a big sticky patch right at the crotch. The scent of her own heat was driving her wild, and the sight of her mate slowly coming to her, cock bouncing like a heavy log, fists clenching as he prepared to manhandle her and put his seed deep into her almost made her give in.

"No," she said, pulling her legs up close and hugging her knees. "We need to hold on. We can't break. Just a little while longer. We can do it."

But Bart was standing above her now, and he reached down and stroked her hair, ran the back of his hand along her cheek. She could feel the roughness of his skin, sense every scar on his hands, perhaps every scar on his body too. She looked up at him, blinking as she saw long marks across his torso.

"Where did these scars come from?" she asked, reaching up and running her finger along three scars

that looked like claw marks. "I thought you said Shifters heal fast."

"We do," said Bart, still stroking her cheek from
above. Finally he looked down at himself and grinned.
"But these scars are from a Shifter. The dragon. Adam
Drake."

Bis frowned. "I thought he was your friend. Your
military brother. You guys had a fight?"

Bart snorted, finally backing off from her and beginning to slowly pace. She could feel a change in his
energy at the mention of Adam Drake and the crew,
and she immediately saw how meaningful that had
been for Bart. Yes, his animal needed its mate. But it
also needed its pack, its tribe, its brothers.

"We fought all the time," Bart said with a smile, the
strained muscles on his neck relaxing as a faraway
look entered his eyes. "Testing each other's strength,
sometimes just releasing some energy. It was wild.
There was one time Caleb tried to get in the middle
of it, and Adam just swiped his tail and sent that wolf
flying thirty feet into the air! We laughed so damned
hard! The flying squirrel, we called him after that.
Hell, Caleb was so damned pissed!"

"Caleb the wolf Shifter," Bis said, smiling as she
watched her mate's eyes light up as he spoke of his
crew. "Where is he? Do you know?"

Bart frowned as if something had occurred to him,
but then he shook his head. "No. Probably out there

somewhere. Caleb was quiet, kept to himself even in the crew. But he was deadly in a fight. Goddamn ruthless. Adam and I were always glad he was on our side. Wolves aren't as big as bears or as powerful as dragons, but they've got their strengths. The flying squirrel incident aside, Caleb could hold his own even against a Shifter ten times his size. Take a look."

Bart stuck out his right leg, pointing at two round scars that looked like teeth marks from large, long, deadly-sharp fangs.

"Ya Allah," Bis muttered, putting her hand over her mouth as she tried not to imagine the beast that could do that to her mate, who seemed all-powerful and invincible. "Your *friend* did that to you?" She shook her head. "Sometimes I don't think I will ever understand how men interact with one another."

Bart laughed again as he slowly strolled around the cage, his chest stuck out wide, head held high. Bis could see the joy he got from talking about his crew, Adam the dragon and Caleb the wolf, and she knew that they were a big part of his life, that even though he'd found his mate, there were parts of him that needed that interaction with his crew, with the boys.

"How about you?" he said, looking down at her, a gentle smile breaking on his taut, lean face. "Tell me about your life, Miss Bis. Your friends. Your family. Anything. Everything!"

Bis blinked, drawing her legs closer to herself as she

felt like she wanted to close up. She'd always been a private person, and this was all new to her: Someone wanting to actually know about her!

"I . . . I don't know what to tell you," she stammered, blinking again. "I don't really have any friends. I mean, I get along fine with the other teachers. Well, most of them, at least. There is this one teacher who's a real bitch to me, though. She always said I thought I was a big-shot because I studied in England and then chose to return to Syria and teach English. She said I was stuck-up and pretentious!"

Bart frowned, twisting his mouth and shaking his head. "Some people are just negative. No big deal. I'll eat her when we get out of here."

Bis howled with surprised laughter as she listened to her mate talk matter-of-factly about eating a teacher for being a bitch. But what surprised her the most was that she knew he might not be joking—and she sort of understood it! "OK, you do *not* eat people anymore. We are *not* going to raise our children like that. We are not that sort of family."

Bart grunted and made a sulky face, like he was pouting for being denied the chance to eat people or teach his kids to do the same. Bis felt her heart fill with a delightful warmth as she tried to understand why it felt so natural to be talking about kids and family with this man—well, half-man—that she'd only just met! They really were fated, weren't they?

And didn't fate mean that everything would work out just fine, that it would all be perfect, that they'd get their happy ending?

"Some people deserve to be eaten," Bart said in that playful sulky tone. "I am most certainly going to eat Murad. And you can eat the witch. Though I bet she'd cause your cat some indigestion."

Bis shrugged, her eyes sparkling as she felt her cat shrug along with her. "I'll take some Rolaids after eating the witch. I should be fine. My digestive system is pretty tough," she said, patting the healthy round of her belly.

Bart laughed, his gaze moving down along her curves and making her tingle all over. "All right, so no friends," he said quickly like he was trying to keep talking just to keep his attention off her body. "What about family?"

Bis sighed and shook her head. "Parents were killed in a bomb blast when I was a teenager. I was an only child, and one of the humanitarian groups got me to England as a refugee. I spent ten years in London before coming back."

Bart nodded. "Why did you go back to Syria? Anyone else would have stayed in England."

Bis shrugged. "I don't know. Felt like I could help, I suppose. Like it was my responsibility. My duty. An obligation." She paused as a strange thought came to her. "Fate."

"Fate," said Bart, his eyes narrowing as he folded his arms across his broad chest. "I like the idea. And it seems to be working so far."

"I don't know if sitting here in a cage as prisoners of a mad Sheikh and a dark witch is proof that fate is working out for us," Bis said, cocking her head and glancing at him sideways.

"We're together, aren't we? That's the only kind of fate guaranteed for Shifters. That you'll find your fated mate." He glanced around at their prison, shrugging once and winking at her. "As far as everything else goes . . . it's all up for discussion."

"Or negotiation," Bis said, feeling her cat go on high alert as the massive wooden door at the far end of the room creaked open. "Speaking of which, it's game on, fated mate."

10

"**F**ated mates who refuse to mate," said the witch Magda, stopping outside the cage and staring curiously at Bart and then Bis. Her pale face was drawn into a tight smile, and Bis swore she saw a genuine look of surprise in the witch's dead black eyes. "This is most certainly a twist." She glanced down at Bart's thick, filled-out manhood and then over at Bis. "Clearly he wants her. And he is still in human form, so she is indeed his mate. Strange. I don't think I've seen anything like it. The few fated Shifter couples that we've managed to capture have mated at the first chance we gave them. But your level of self-control is admirable. So admirable that I might actually be willing to give your proposal some thought."

"You cannot be serious," said Sheikh Murad, striding across the room and slamming the door closed as if he didn't want anyone else to hear. Bis sniffed the air, wondering why he was worried about his guards overhearing. Was there someone else out there? She thought she picked up the scent of an animal—perhaps a wolf? She didn't know, though. She'd never smelled a wolf before. Maybe the mention of Caleb the wolf had wolves on her mind.

"Well, these two are most certainly serious," Magda said without turning to the Sheikh. "I know you are skeptical about fated mates, but the fact that they have been able to hold off from mating is extraordinary. We should consider their proposal. They could be useful. They could be leaders as we build my Shifter army. Not just average Shifters that we keep in cages and breed like the animals they are."

"I thought it was *my* army," Murad said under his breath, his gold eyes blazing with an anger that told Bis that there were hints of tension between these two. "And if they have so much self-control and intelligence, the *last* thing I want is to let them out of their cage! Leave them, Magda. Stop giving them food. Sooner or later they will either fuck each other or eat each other." He glanced disdainfully at Bis and then Bart. "That is my counter-proposal, you flea-infested freaks. Mate and deliver me your offspring, or else starve until one of you eats the other."

"Delivering you our offspring is exactly what we're

proposing," said Bart, his arms crossed over his chest, cock hanging down like he didn't give a damn. Bis almost smiled at how confident her man was while standing naked in a cage, and she felt like together they could do anything! Maybe Magda was right: They *were* special! Fated for more than just mating like animals!

"Yes," Bis said. "We just want to also deliver you *ourselves* along with our children. We want to hold our family together. Nothing else matters to us. We're single-minded and focused. Let us be with our kids, and we'll join you in whatever plans you've got. Our animals will submit to us so long as their mates are together and they are able to protect and raise their offspring. It's the most basic drive of life, and everything else is secondary."

Murad snorted. "You two will eat us the first chance you get. I'm not a fool, even though you seem to have gotten through to Magda." He glared at the witch. "Remind me not to send you into any more negotiations on my behalf."

"We don't *eat* people," said Bis hotly. "We're not those sort of Shifters, and we're not going to be that sort of family."

Murad burst into laughter as Magda raised both thin black eyebrows at Bis.

"Not *those* sort of Shifters?! My, my, we have a sophisticated, cultured, well-mannered monster here, don't we?" said Murad, still laughing like the madman he was. Abruptly he stopped the laughter, further proving that he was crazy—at least in Bis's opinion. "Look, lady, there is only one kind of Shifter: The kind that wants to do nothing but kill, feed, and fuck. Besides, you're of no use to me if you're going to refuse to kill. I'm starting an army here, not a book-club."

"Book club isn't a bad idea," Bis retorted, almost kicking herself for getting into a nonsensical argument with a lunatic. But she couldn't help herself. This guy was an arsehole, and she wasn't going to take it. "Though I bet you can't even read, you're so bug-eyed from your craziness. I'm surprised you aren't frothing at the mouth," she muttered, half under her breath but certainly loud enough for everyone to hear.

From the corner of her eye she saw Bart flinch and stare at her like he thought *she* was the crazy one. Murad's dark face had turned a deep shade of red, and for a moment Bis worried that he would in fact start frothing at the mouth! She almost giggled when she realized she'd gotten to him with nothing but a few casual insults, and it gave her a boost of confidence—a perverse sort of confidence, but confidence nonetheless.

"What's the matter, Sheikh Madman—I mean Murad," she whispered, stepping close to the bars of the cage and narrowing her eyes at him. "Cat got your tongue? Meow."

With a roar the Sheikh leapt forward, spreading his arms out wide like they were wings, his gold eyes burning like fire. He crashed against the bars of the cage with such force that the entire room seemed to shake, and Bis swore he would have broken through if Magda the witch hadn't suddenly uttered some incomprehensible words that seemed to stop Murad's attack.

"*Lethorum ilsum drakonica*," she whispered, her eyes rolling up in her head, a thick vein bulging at her neck as if she was expending a huge amount of energy. "*Nolena wyree drakonica.*"

The Sheikh's black robe glowed with an eerie light as he fell to the floor gasping. Bis stared in shock, trying to process what had just happened. She didn't understand the language the witch was using, but the word *drakonica* sounded too much like *dragon* to be ignored. Of course! The man was Adam Drake's father, wasn't he? He was a dragon, and Bis had pissed him off so much that the rage of the dragon had almost got him to Change! In fact he *would* have Changed if the witch hadn't held him back with her dark magic—magic that clearly put some strain on her. Made sense. It must take serious energy to stop a dragon Shifter from Changing.

The wheels began to turn in Bis's mind as she took in the new information, absorbing it like a sponge, her intelligence feeling sharp, her cat-powers at the

fullest. Cat powers? Sure. Why not. There were witch-
es, dragons, and bears in the room as it was. This was
the world in which she played now.

But she wasn't going to play with Murad any longer. What she'd seen had scared her. She thought back
to the life-changing sight of his son Adam swooping
down from the heavens, his gold-and-green wings
flashing in the sunlight, his gigantic maws open
wide as he spewed fire and dispensed death. Adam
had saved her and the girls, but the power he'd pro-
jected was still terrifying. What kind of power did
Drake the Elder possess? What kind of dragon would
Sheikh Murad be? Murad Drake? Was that even his
real name? Didn't sound right.

Bis blinked as she watched Magda lead the Sheikh
from the room. His robe was still glowing, but his
eyes had lost their fire. What was up with these two?
Who was controlling whom here?

The door slammed shut and suddenly they were
alone again as an awful chill settled over Bis.

"Oh, God, I ruined everything with my big fat
mouth!" she said, turning to Bart in despair. "I don't
know what came over me! I'm sorry! I just . . ."

Bart shrugged, his lips trembling as he held back
a smile. "I thought it was funny. Cat got your tongue
was a good line."

Bis snorted, closing her eyes and shaking her head.

"It isn't funny, Bart! We were supposed to have a serious negotiation, and I screwed it up by losing my cool."

"You seemed pretty cool to me, Miss Bis," said Bart. "Old man dragon was the one who lost his cool."

"I know!" said Bis, her eyes going wide. "I forgot he was a dragon! If he'd Changed, I don't know what would have happened."

Bart grunted, every muscle on his body suddenly tightening as if in reflex to even the suggestion that his mate might have been hurt. "You have nothing to worry about when I'm with you. I've fought a dragon before, and I'm still here. A bit of singed fur and a couple of scars, sure. But I would protect you with my life, Miss Bis."

"Miss Bis," said Bismeeta, feeling that warmth flow through her body like the desert breeze. Even though they were in a cage, embroiled in a situation that was crazy at best, deadly at worst, she felt what could only be described as joy! Shit, she was *happy*! How did that even make sense! "I like that. I could get used to it."

"Well, don't get too used to it, Miss Bis," said Bart, stepping close and playing with her long black hair, opening up a knot that had formed, his thick fingers displaying remarkable gentleness and precision. She blinked as she tried to push away the thought of those fingers playing with another part of her body, shaking her head when she noted that he'd been shamelessly naked all this while, with a chub the size of a *halaal* beef sausage.

"Why shouldn't I get used to it?" she demanded playfully. "You going somewhere? Leaving me already?"

"On the contrary, Miss Bis," he said softly, "I ain't going nowhere. Not now. Not ever. I'm just reminding you that soon you're gonna be *Mrs.* Bis."

"Missus Bissus," muttered Bis, looking up into his eyes as he stroked her hair. She wanted him to kiss her, and she could see the need in his eyes. But they had to play their game, stick to their guns, restrain themselves as they negotiated their way out of this cage. "I could get used to that too. You think Sheikh Murad is ordained to marry us?"

Bart snorted. "I doubt he's even a real Sheikh. I don't remember Adam saying anything about being royalty." He paused, that wistful look returning to his eyes as he talked about his old crew. "Though Adam didn't talk much about himself."

"You said Caleb was quiet too. So wait, does that mean you were the talkative one in the group?" Bis said, opening her mouth wide as she let out a squeal. "Oh, that's rich. I feel sorry for those guys."

"Did you just insult me?" Bart demanded, putting his hands on his muscular hips and glaring at her, his brown eyes twinkling. "I think I've just been insulted by a cat!"

"*Big* cat," said Bis. "You called me a *big* cat, remember. That was the first insult of the day."

"You are a big cat," Bart said, coming close, so close she trembled as she felt the heat of his body. "Big and beautiful and mine. All mine. Come here."

"No," she whispered, laughing and backing away. It felt like they were flirting, playing, two fated lovers on a first date. But they were also in a cage, trying to hold their own against a dragon gone bad and a witch who'd perhaps never been good. Why was this so much fun?! Was this what it was like to go insane?

"The cameras are still off," Bart growled, and she blinked as he went fully hard like he was going to take her now, strategy and plans be damned. "They won't even know."

"Unless I get pregnant," said Bis, backing away playfully as he came slowly for her, cock leading the way. "And then they'll know we can't control ourselves around each other, which means they don't need to listen to a thing we say. They can just breed us like animals, take our children every year."

"They could do that anyway," Bart said. "This plan isn't gonna work, Bis. They could just lie and say sure, they'll agree to everything we say, that they believe that we'd be willing to join them if we get to keep our children, keep our family together. And then once you pop out a litter of kittens or a brood of cubs, we're back in the cage and they just shrug and say thank you very much."

Bis closed her eyes and sighed. Bart was probably right. Who was she kidding. They didn't have any leverage, did they? But wait. What did Magda the witch say to Murad before they left the room? Wasn't she genuinely impressed that Bis and Bart hadn't gone to town on each other when they were left alone? Yes, she was. Which meant the wheels were turning in the witch's head. The witch saw some use for these two. The only sticking point would be trust. No way the witch would trust that they were just going to join her and Murad in their plans.

Not unless Bis and Bart gave the witch a reason to trust them.

"What do you know about dark magic?" Bis said suddenly as goosebumps popped up all over her smooth brown skin, the tiny hairs at the back of her neck rising to attention.

Bart frowned, and then he shook his head and shrugged. "Not much. The witch uses it—that much is clear." He glanced at the shining metal bars. "She's used it on this cage to make it indestructible—by me at least. She uses it on Murad through his cloak to stop him from Changing into a dragon. So she's powerful. Her dark magic is serious shit."

"Yes, but she's got her limits, doesn't she? After all, she couldn't use it to Change you back to a human."

"No," said Bart, raising an eyebrow and glancing down at her breasts. "That took a different kind of magic. Speaking of breasts, I'm just gonna touch the left one. Just suck on your nipple a bit. Just a taste."

"Um, we were *not* speaking of breasts, you animal!" said Bis, giggling as she covered her boobs with her arms. "And my breasts don't *taste* like anything! I don't think so, at least," she added, frowning as she sniffed her underarms and then wrinkled up her nose. "Well, maybe they'll taste a bit salty since I haven't showered in . . . OK, stop! Do *not* derail this conversation by talking about my boobs!"

"I won't talk at all if you let me do what I want," said Bart, grinning wide as he sauntered towards her like they were in the honeymoon suite at the Ritz Carlton in Piccadilly. "Just the left one."

Bis laughed again as a hot wave of pure arousal washed through her. She hugged herself, backing away from him playfully as he bore down on her in their cage. "Why the left one?" she said, giggling as she looked down at herself. "Is it bigger? Oh, God, are my boobs not the same size?! Am I a hideous freak with mismatched boobs?!"

"Hmmm," said Bart, rubbing his square jaw. "Mismatched boobs could be a serious issue. I'll need to inspect both breasts to make sure. Here. Let me see."

He was on her now, and he pulled her arms away with such ease that she gasped at his strength. Yes, he was big and muscular, broad and hard, but she was still shocked at just how powerful he was. And this was as a human! Imagine his strength when he let his bear take control!

Her cat purred in delight as Bart held her arms out wide, pushing her against the bars of the cage as his cock stuck straight out like a post, its massive shaft lodging itself right between her legs like they'd been designed to fit together. She groaned as she felt her wetness ooze down the insides of her thighs, and now she knew she was powerless, that she was going to submit, give in, let him take her.

"We can't," she muttered, her eyelids fluttering as she felt his hot breath on her bare neck. "Bart, listen. There's a chance here. There's something about this witch's magic that is going to work to our benefit. She's not all-powerful, or else she could just cast some spell to make us do exactly what she wants."

"Who gives a rat's ass about some witch," Bart growled, leaning in and sniffing her neck, panting as he breathed deep of her scent. "Who gives a rat's ass about anything?! I am all-powerful right now. You make me feel my own power, Bis. All of it. Power like I've never felt. You're mine, and once I take you, I'm gonna bust through these bars, storm through the walls, break through the gates. Trust me, honey, no witch, dragon, or army is gonna stop me once I've claimed you as mine."

"All right, maybe you will be strong enough to destroy everything and everyone once you get what you want—what we *both* want," Bis said, trying desperately to think as she felt his thick shaft slide against her wet slit from beneath. Her robe was soaked at the crotch, and she knew she wouldn't be able to talk much longer, that this was going to happen if she didn't find a way to get him to back down. She had to be the one to control their arousal, because he sure as hell wasn't going to be able to do it. "But then what? What if you do break free, get the two of us out of here? What then?"

Bart pulled back and looked down at her like she was crazy for even asking the question. "Isn't it obvious, Miss Bis? I mean, Missus Bissus. We mate all day and all night for a hundred years. End of story."

Bis laughed and shook her head. "You've just got lust on the brain right now. You know that won't make you happy in the long run. There's more to you than that."

"I don't think so," growled Bart, licking her neck slowly as she shuddered. "Damn, you taste good. So fucking good, Bis."

"There is," she whispered, her eyes rolling up in her head as the arousal threatened to break her will, break her resolve, break everything in her. "I've seen how you talk about your crew, your military brothers. And why did you even join the Army to begin with? There's a need inside you, a need to make a difference, to use your strength and power for good, for justice, for . . ."

But he kissed her full on the mouth just then, and

she gasped as his lips smothered hers. Everything in her wanted to kiss him back, to just give in, give up, submit to his strength. But she pulled her head back and turned away from him even as her animal roared in displeasure.

Bart's grip on her wrists tightened, and now he was pushing against her so hard she could feel the bars digging into her backside. He tried to kiss her again, but she shook her head furiously, fighting her arousal, fighting her animal, fighting her mate. Her animal was hissing in the background as her arousal screamed through her shuddering body, and for a moment she couldn't even remember why she was fighting this. He was her mate, and they were meant to be, so why resist?

"Please," she groaned as Bart leaned in once more, his body pressed tight against hers. "We need to hold on, Bart. For the sake of our children. Our future. Our *family*!"

With a shout of pure anguish Bart pulled away from her, releasing her wrists and then slamming his open palms against the bars of the cage, making the entire structure rattle and shake. Bis gasped as she felt his weight move off her, her chest heaving as she took deep gulping breaths. Her animal was mewing inside, fighting to get out like it wanted to finish this on its own.

"All right!" Bart shouted, punching the metal bars so hard Bis didn't understand how every bone in his hand didn't shatter. "God dammit, all *right*! I'm listening, Bis. But make it quick. And make it convincing."

11

"**O**K, I've listened, but I'm still not convinced," Bart said stubbornly, narrowing his eyes as he stared at his even more stubborn mate. His bear was going crazy inside, growling, rumbling, and pawing to be let out.

"Well, I'm convinced I'm right," said Bis. "Magda's magic needs something to latch onto for it to work. Her dark magic needs to find something dark inside us for it to work on us. That's why she can't just cast a spell and have us do anything she wants. It works on Murad because there's a darkness inside him that hates his own dragon, and so her magic is able to stop him from Changing. The magic has to use something that's already inside the other person."

"Maybe you're right. But how does that change

anything for us? If there was something inside us that the witch could use, she'd have done it by now, wouldn't she?"

Bis shrugged, her face hardening for a moment in a way that made Bart frown. "Maybe it was buried too deep. Maybe we need to find it on our own first, bring it out, offer it to Magda as a way in. Perhaps our leverage here is to actually *give up* leverage!"

"Offer Magda a way in . . ." Bart repeated. "You're saying you want to open yourself up to the witch's dark magic? Have me do the same? Are you crazy? Do you know anything about dark magic?"

Bis shrugged again. "Only what I've read."

"What you've *read*?! Shit, I forgot I was talking to a teacher here. Educated woman. I didn't even finish high school! All right. Hit me with it. What treatise on Dark Magic did you read? A thousand-page book with an old leather cover that you found in an attic in London?"

"No, I read about it in a paranormal romance novel," Bis said, her eyebrows rising innocently as she looked into Bart's eyes. "And what I've seen of Magda seems to back up what I've read. I'm confident I'm right."

Bart's mouth hung open as he tried to figure out if this woman was serious or if she'd lost her mind because of the stress. But she seemed calm, collected, even excited. Perhaps it was a different sort of crazy, something he hadn't seen.

"So you're basing our entire strategy on some crap

you read in a cheesy romance novel?" he growled, shaking his head like there was water in his ears. "Great. My mate is insane. Out of her damned mind."

"Why? Isn't our entire story just the plotline of a romance novel?" she said, her eyes shining as a smile broke on her brown face. "Fated mates, brought together by coincidence, facing obstacles together as they fight for their happily ever after . . . *so* romantic!"

Bart snorted, still shaking his head. "Your delusional imagination is the only obstacle I see in the way of our happily ever after," he muttered, glancing down at her breasts and feeling his heart pound in his chest as images of him sucking her nipples flooded his overheated brain. Damn, he wanted her. Why was he still even talking?! He should have taken her ten times by now, emptied himself in her again and again, shut her damned mouth with his kisses, spanked her big round bottom until she squealed in submission! Yet here he was negotiating with her about how to negotiate with some other crazy people! He wasn't cut out for this sort of complexity! He was the muscle! The brute force! He should be roaming free in the forests with his mate, taking her sex whenever he wanted—which would be *all* the time. Day and night. Again and again. God, what the hell was he waiting for?! Enough of this nonsense! We're done. We're just—

Listen to her, whispered his bear from the inside. *She*

sees things you don't, you big lug. She understands the witch, understands how her magic works. Listen to your mate on this one.

"Wait, *you* are asking me to hold off from taking my mate, from *mating* with her?!" Bart shouted, not even bothering to keep his voice low. "Shut up, you self-righteous, treacherous furball! I'm in control here!"

"Wait, what's happening?" Bis demanded, putting her hands on her hips and staring up at him with wide eyes. "Are you seriously debating with your animal about how and when to *mate* me? You realize that the choice is mine, not yours, don't you?"

Bart's eyes narrowed as his mind swirled. There was suddenly so much going on. His bear whispering advice from the inside. His mate berating him from the outside. He didn't have patience for this shit. *Her* choice?! Fuck, he'd show her how much choice she had when she was face down and spread wide for him, taking everything he could give as he pounded her ass raw, filling her with his seed until she overflowed!

He almost roared in anguish as he felt his bear resist when not so long ago his bear just wanted to mate! Again the bear whispered that they needed to listen to her, that their time would come, that fate would play out in its own way. It almost made him lose his mind, but Bart knew he couldn't ignore his bear's words. They connected with something he saw in Bis's eyes, heard in her voice. She was smart in a way he wasn't—book smart, studious, scholarly. Bart had his own intelligence that played out in the forest, on the hunt, in a fight. But this was his mate's domain: The delicate art of diplomacy, the tactics of talking your way out of something when your physical strength is neutralized. She was his complement, his missing piece. She completed him, and he had to let it ride, let her lead when she was in her domain.

"All right," he said, his eyes still flashing with impatience as he swallowed hard. He glanced up and down along her curves, licking his lips as he fought for control. "So you want us to . . . what *do* you want us to do? Offer ourselves to the witch? Tell her to cast her spells on us or some shit?"

Bis frowned like she was thinking. "I don't think we'll need to tell her anything. She's probably been looking for a way to bring us under her dark spells anyway. We just need to give her that way in. Find that darkness inside us, give it some space to breathe, to grow."

"OK, I'm just a bear. I don't even understand what that means," Bart grumbled. "Give it space to breathe? Sounds hokey and dumb."

"Can we hold off on passing judgment for just one damned moment?" Bis said, taking an annoyed breath as she blinked and looked down at the sandstone floor. She went silent, her chest moving as she breathed slow and deep. Then she slowly looked up.

"All right," she said quietly. "Here's what we need to do, Bart. Think about the proposal we made to Murad and Magda. What did we say we were going to do?"

Bart shrugged. He wanted to sulk, but he forced himself to humor her. "That we were willing to join their dumbass evil plans as long as we weren't separated from each other or from our yet-to-be-born children." He raised an eyebrow. "Yet to be *conceived* children, I might add. Talk about putting the cart before the horse." A grin later he was striding towards her again. "So perhaps we need to solve that problem right away. Put the horse in front of the cart. Put my baby inside of you."

"Bart, listen, we're almost there! Please, listen!" she said, backing away from him again and going up flush against the cage bars.

But Bart couldn't hear a thing. This was too much thinking, too much talking. He knew what his body wanted, and he was a man who lived in the flesh, in the physical. The bear tried to resist for a moment, but the scent of its mate was too much, the sight of her smooth brown skin too tempting. Suddenly he was all animal again, all lust and passion, need and desire. He knew this was going to happen. He'd held off as long as he could, but now it was pointless to hold back. To hell with plans. To hell with strategy. It was time to do what nature ordained. It was time to take his mate. Let fate sort out the rest.

12

Fate can only work through people and their choices, Bis told herself as she moved along the walls of the cage, doing her best to stay away from him, this gigantic beast of a man who'd been naked the entire time she'd known him. She was his, she knew. And God, she wanted to give herself to him. But they were also a team, also a part of something bigger that was happening here. She knew it, and she had to follow those instincts as much as the instinct to just say to hell with it and mate like her animal wanted.

Bart was closing in on her, but just then she heard the click of the door closing at the far end of the room. It was Magda the witch. Bis could feel her presence, smell her scent, sense her darkness even before she saw the woman. The witch was alone, and she'd come in quietly and was just standing there, her black eyes shining with dark light, the kind of light that sucks energy out of the world.

"Look inside yourself, Bart," Bis whispered as she felt a chill rise up along her back as her mate came close. He was so focused on her that he hadn't heard Magda come in, and Bis blinked as she realized that this was the moment, this was when it needed to happen, this was her chance to pull herself and her mate deeper into this—pull them deeper because it was their best chance of making it out at the end of it.

"I'm looking, but all I can see is you," Bart growled, brushing a strand of hair from her face and then reaching around to the back of her neck and clamping down hard with his fingers. "All I can smell is your scent. All I can hear is your heart pounding in rhythm with mine."

Bis blinked as she suddenly became conscious of her heart. She took a slow breath, frowning as she put her soft hand against her mate's broad chest. The sound of his mighty heart almost deafened her as she felt it rock her body just from the contact.

"Oh, God," she muttered, blinking again and then looking up into his eyes. "Our hearts are beating in time, Bart. In perfect sync. Like it's one heart. Like we share a heart."

She almost lost her train of thought as Bart grunted and lowered his face to her hair, breathing deep as he inhaled her scent. He held her neck tight with one hand, the other reaching behind her as he let his thick fingers trace their way down the middle of her back, all the way down over the curve of her bottom, teasing her by drawing little circles on her sturdy buttcheeks with his fingertips as her wetness oozed down the inside of her thighs.

"What would you do for me?" she whispered as the arousal snaked its way through her body. "To protect me, to protect the children we're going to have, to raise them together, to be a family, a family forever."

"Anything," Bart whispered into her hair. "Everything."

"Me too," Bis whispered, her eyelids fluttering open as she saw the witch Magda tense up across the room, her slim frame convulsing like she was going into a trance or having a seizure or something. Fear and doubt rose up in Bis like twin snakes as she felt Bart's breath against her forehead, his grip tightening on her neck, his fingers slowly teasing her rear as he pulled at her gown. She could feel his rock-hard erection pressing against her mound, its length reaching all the way up past her belly-button as he began to slowly grind against her. He was consumed by his arousal, oblivious to everything and anything. He was being honest when he said he'd do anything and everything for her, for his mate, his family, his bloodline. She would too, and this was something she needed to do, no matter how much it scared her. There was darkness in everyone, just like there was an animal in every human, Shifter or not. Bis just had to trust that the light in her and her mate would ultimately win out. It had to! They were both good people, weren't they? She'd returned to Syria from a life of ease in England to help her war-torn country. He'd joined the U.S. Army so he could channel his strength to do some good in the world. Those were honorable, selfless motives, and those needs were still alive in both of them, weren't they? They couldn't just turn their backs on whatever was happening here with Magda and Murad. They had to fight, and the only way was to go in deeper, to get closer to the enemy, to become part of the darkness and trust that their own light would prevent them from being lost to the darkness forever.

"Me too," Bis whispered again as Bart reached down with both hands and cupped her ass so hard she groaned. "I'd do anything for you, for our children, for our family. Fight, kill, destroy. Lie, cheat, steal. Anything."

Bart nodded against her as Bis saw the witch's eyelids begin to flutter. Bis knew Magda was summoning her dark power to harness the darkness in Bis and Bart—a darkness rooted in the raw instinct to mate, to protect their young, to protect their family.

"We'd do anything," Bis whispered, feeling her body tingle as the witch's lips began to move, silent words being uttered from across the room. "Say it, Bart. Anything for each other. No one else matters. Nothing else matters."

"Anything," Bart growled, his hands ripping open her gown from behind, his fingers clawing at her bare skin as he pushed her up against the bars of their cage. "Anything for you. Anything for us. Anything for *this*!"

The witch's eyes flicked wide open just as Bart said the words, and Bis gasped when she saw that Magda's eyes were all black, shining like black pearls on a moonlit night. The witch's body was firm as a rail, dark blue veins pulsating all over her pale face as she whispered her secret words and stared with those dark, dead eyes.

Then suddenly Magda hunched over, letting out a shuddering breath as she staggered forward. She almost fell to the floor, but then she straightened up to her full height again, her chest heaving as she gulped air. For a moment Bis thought that perhaps the witch had failed, that maybe her spells wouldn't work on them, that maybe the plan was dumb, that she and Bart were doomed to be locked in a cage so they could pop out babies every year like lab monkeys. But then Magda's thin lips tightened into a smile, and with a twirl of her robe she left the room.

"Oh, God," Bis muttered as she felt something change inside her, her mind suddenly getting flooded with images of she and her mate fighting together, hunting together, killing together, Magda and Murad watching from the background like puppet masters. "Oh, God, Bart, I think I just . . . I think I might have made a terrible mistake. I might have seriously done something that . . . that . . ."

But she couldn't finish the sentence, because Bart had ripped the rest of her gown off her shoulders, the cold bars of their cage pressing into her naked back as her mate grabbed her hair from behind and looked down into her eyes.

"Oh, God, I'm sorry, Bart," she groaned as tears rolled down her cheeks. Now she knew she'd screwed up, made a mistake that might destroy them forever, perhaps destroy many others along with it. She saw it in his eyes, and the realization dawned on her that although she knew Bart was fundamentally good-hearted, there was a lot of darkness, conflict, and turmoil in him too. She'd given that part of him free rein to come out by reminding him that he'd do anything for his mate, and the witch's magic had latched onto it with glee. She touched his face as she looked into his sunken eyes, and then she nodded as she understood that there was no turning back now. He was her mate, and she'd have to stay with him, follow him wherever this choice would lead them. She could feel the witch's magic taking hold even as her mind swirled, and now she understood that tight smile of superiority on Magda's face as she left the room. "Bart, I'm so . . . so—"

And then everything went blank as Bis felt the magic envelop the two of them like a blanket, and she just opened her mouth as Bart leaned in and kissed her so hard she could taste the blood on her lips. Blood both hers and his. Their fate sealed with a kiss.

He kissed her again and again, hard and with a hunger that scared her even as her arousal whipped around inside her like a snake on fire. Those images of the future came roaring back as she kissed her mate, images of babies and blood, chaos and cuddling, fighting and fucking, death and diapers, light and darkness all mixed up, good and evil bubbling together in an invisible cauldron.

"I want to consume you, Bis," Bart growled against her cheek as he licked her face, kissed her again, and then dropped to his knees and buried his face between her legs. "Taste you, smell you, swallow you. All of you."

"Do it," she groaned, grabbing the bars of the cage as Bart held her thighs apart and began to lick her between her legs, his tongue parting her matted black curls, finding her slit and sliding in so quickly she screamed in shock. "Drink from me. Taste me."

His tongue curled up inside her vagina as she said words that should have shocked her but were instead taking her arousal to dizzying heights, and as Bart reached around from behind and parted her rear globes, pulling her hips hard into his face, she felt herself come like she didn't think was possible.

Bis snapped her head back and screamed as she felt her wetness pour down all over her mate's face, and she could feel him slurp and swallow as he took her with his tongue. Her head was pounding from the force with which she'd hit the metal cage, her body shaking from the climax rocking her from the inside, her mind a twisted mess as more images of the future came rolling in like storm waves crashing against the shore.

She felt Bart pull her down to the cold sandstone floor, down to her knees as he rose up and kissed her full on the lips again. She could feel her own juices on his lips and face, smell her own sex on his stubble, taste her own tangy sweetness on his tongue as she kissed him back. She could feel herself smiling as she let those images roll through her mind without resistance, images of her as an animal, a big cat with claws drawn, running alongside her beast of a mate, Bart in all his animal glory, the two of them running wild, wreaking havoc, sowing destruction throughout the desert, letting the darkest parts of them take control. Was this the witch's magic at work, or was it just Bis herself? Perhaps she didn't know herself at all! Perhaps all that self-righteousness when she'd

chosen to return to Syria to "help the children" was
bullshit! Maybe . . . maybe . . .

She gasped as Bart suddenly grabbed her hair and
flipped her around, pushing her down face-first and
raising her ass towards his face. She screamed as he
spanked her rear so hard it sounded like rifle shots in
the empty room, his open palms coming down flat on
her asscheeks left and right as he roared in delight.

He rubbed her between her legs, his fingers roughly flicking her clit from beneath as she panted from
the shock of being spanked like that. Her ass was
stinging, but it felt sickeningly good, she had to admit. Bis moaned out loud and then grinned as she
felt him massage her large buttocks before slapping
each rear cheek again until she felt her heavy globes
shudder in response.

"You are divine," he growled from behind her, and
Bis could feel the warm desert air swirl around her
as he spread her asscheeks so wide it hurt. "Perfect
and round. Clean like a whistle."

Bismeeta's eyes rolled up in her head as she felt
Bart's tongue slowly move down her crack, teasing
her rear pucker in a way that felt so filthy she almost
came again. She was spread so wide even her slit was
open and stretched, its wetness dripping in heavy
beads like condensation on a humid night.

"Ya Allah, what are you doing," she muttered as he
gently slapped each buttcheek again and then spat
on her asshole before firmly placing his thumb right

there. "Oh, please don't. I don't think I can . . . I don't know if I can . . . I . . . I . . . I . . . oh, oh, *oh!*"

She swallowed her words as Bart twisted his thumb slowly into her rear hole like he was driving in a corkscrew, and it was all she could do to not pass out from the sheer ecstasy of being penetrated like that. Her entire body was tingling, and she swore she was giving off the same kind of light that infused the bars of the cage they were in.

If this is dark magic, then bring it on, she thought as she felt another climax begin to roll in as her mate pulled his thumb out of her, licked her wet hole, and then slid his thick, long middle finger into that dark space as he lined his cockhead up against her parted slit from below. She felt powerless under his grip: beautifully powerless, magically powerless, powerless and weightless, like a burden was being lifted off her—the burden of morality, expectations, right and wrong. Nothing mattered but him. Nothing but how good it felt to be taken, claimed, mated. That was the only meaning in life. Everything else could go jump off a bridge.

And as Bart slowly pushed his massive, throbbing shaft past the lips of her vagina and deep into her secret space, opening her up as if for the first time, Bis was certain this was right, this was perfect, this was everything. Pleasure was everything, wasn't it? What more was there to life? They were animals, after all. Built to mate, built to give birth, built to pro-

tect their young so the next generation could do the same! Life in a nutshell! Why did humans need to make it so complicated?!

Bart rammed the last few inches of his manhood into her just as she felt that second climax roar in like a tidal wave of ecstasy, and she screamed as she felt his finger curl up in her rear as he held her firmly down and began to pump.

"Oh, you're in so deep," she groaned, her eyes rendered sightless as she gasped for air, the waves of her climax crashing in again and again as Bart rammed into her, pushing his long, thick cock so far inside her she swore it was opening up new space in her depths.

Bart didn't reply, and she could barely hear him breathe as he took her from behind, his powerful haunches driving so hard she was convulsing from the force. Her boobs were swinging back and forth as he slammed his hips into her rear cushion with each thrust, twisting that finger in her rear, his other hand gripping the back of her neck and holding her in position.

Finally her climax reached its peak and shattered into a million invisible splinters of pure pleasure, making Bis howl as she hunched her body and almost choked as the ecstasy wound its way slowly down, leaving her head thrumming as her mate kept going. Then through her moans she could finally hear his heart. It was beating like a bass drum, heavy and loud, still in perfect rhythm with hers. She tried to turn and look at him, but his hand was on the back of her neck and he was so strong she was completely at his mercy. For a moment a splinter of fear stabbed her as she wondered what the dark magic was doing to him, if she was in some sort of danger! But then she heard their hearts beat together again in perfect harmony through the chaos of their thrashing bodies, and she felt the fear transform into joy. Pure joy, supreme exhilaration, simple ecstasy, and she laughed like a maniac when she realized that dark magic or not, he was hers and she was his. She would always be safe with him, no matter what they did, no matter what power was cast over their lives. Nothing could get between fated mates.

Nothing except their own choices, came the afterthought as she finally heard Bart begin to pant loudly as his thrusts got wilder and more erratic like he was getting to his own massive climax.

Please let this be the right choice, she prayed as she felt the witch's dark magic swirl through them both as Bart prepared to deliver his seed into her depths. She wasn't sure whom she was praying to. God? The angels? Some other powers out there? Had she been forsaken now that she'd chosed to allow the witch's dark magic to take root in them, to give their own darkness space to grow?

So what if I've been forsaken, she thought firmly

as a strange confidence flowed through her shuddering body as Bart's shouts of pleasure filled the air. All it means is that it's up to me to make sure we navigate this dangerous path correctly. My mate will protect us, protect me, protect the children we have. But I'll have to be the one to make sure we can accept our darkness without losing our connection to what's good and true in us, without losing our connection to the light. Isn't that what being a Shifter is all about? Accepting the animal without losing the human? Finding balance between the flesh and the spirit? Letting the darkness coexist with the light? The witch's magic can only work so long as our inner darkness is out of balance with our natural light. So bring it on. Bring on the darkness, because that might be what it takes to make our light shine brightest.

13

All the light in the room was gone, and Bart was aware of nothing but pleasure, nothing but the feeling of himself deep inside his mate, penetrating her from beneath and behind. The smell of her sex filled his nostrils, and he breathed deep as her scent only increased his arousal. His balls felt heavy and full as he pumped into her, their weight slapping against her underside as he thrust with all the power he had, years of pent-up desire being unleashed in a manic drive to possess her, claim her, take her.

"Am I hurting you?" he managed to mumble through his gritted teeth as he felt the beads of sweat roll down his naked chest and onto her convulsing ass. He could see his middle finger lost inside her rear hole, pushed in all the way down to the knuckle. His cock was so deep inside her, its girth pushing open the walls of her vagina in a way that made her feel so damned tight around him he could barely contain his pleasure. She was magnificent, he thought as he finally saw her beautiful brown body spread before him, her strong hourglass figure so perfect, her curves looking like they'd been sculpted just for him. He'd spanked her bottom, pulled her hair, rammed into her so hard he was worried he'd break her in two. But she was taking everything he had, her body opening up for him, rising to his every need in a way that made him want to yell in delight.

"Bis," he groaned as he pulled back halfway, gasping at the sight of his thick cock sliding out of her, his shaft glistening with her juices. He pushed himself back into her, flexing as his cockhead dragged against the back wall of her vagina. "You need to let me know if I'm hurting you. I'm lost in you, out of my goddamn mind with how this feels, and I might be . . . oh, damn, that feels good! Oh, hell, Bis. You're so damned warm inside. So tight around my cock. Bis, tell me if I'm . . ."

He couldn't finish the sentence as his vision blurred again. Regardless, Bis didn't reply, and it took a moment for Bart to realize that shit, she was coming! Coming hard, coming hot, coming for him! He shouted in delight, pumping harder into her when he realized that she was his mate, that he couldn't hurt her no matter what, that they were made for each other, that he could lose control with her and it would be all right! He could be himself, let the animal in him power his thrusts, let the man in him enjoy her warmth, her heat, her sex, her love.

Again the room went dark as he felt his balls begin to tighten as she screamed and tightened her pussy around his cock, clenching her ass as he drove his finger into her rear canal, her orgasm rocking her body like an earthquake as the cage rattled around them. Bart could sense the bars of the cage glowing with that dark light, and he frowned when he blinked and saw that both he and Bis were bathed in that same strange light.

Then in a rush it all came back to him: What Bis had said about opening themselves up to the witch's dark magic, about how by acknowledging the bit of darkness in themselves they would give Magda a foothold to cast her spells on them! Was that what was happening?! He hadn't seen or heard the witch enter the room, but he'd been so damned focused on his mate that he wouldn't have noticed anyone else, man or beast, angel or demon!

He loosened his grip on the back of Bis's neck, and as she turned her head sideways and glanced at him, he was shocked to see how dark her eyes looked. She'd had beautiful, light brown eyes, but now they were almost black, with a red glow deep in their core! It reminded him of that hazy memory of the wolf's eyes when he'd been captured in South America, and Bart frowned as both fear and rage whipped through him with a suddenness that made him choke.

His body was still pumping as his mind swirled, and now Bart could feel the dark magic winding its way through him like a drug in his veins, slowly taking over from the inside, its black fingers seeking out the darkness that lay within him, forming bonds that seemed both chemical and spiritual.

"What have we done?" Bart groaned as he felt his cock throb as it prepared to deliver his load into his mate. "Bis, you don't know me. You don't know what I've done, what I'm capable of doing, what darkness I've struggled to control for years. I've killed, I've fed, I've destroyed!"

Bis didn't reply, and as Bart's mind whipped itself into a fury with every pump and thrust, he wondered if it was all a trick, if Bis was working with Murad and Magda, if they'd all conspired together to get the dumb bear to walk right into a trap, to willingly surrender to their diabolic schemes! He almost laughed as he thought that it was something that John Benson would have come up with—hell, perhaps it was Benson's idea to begin with! Who the hell knew what was going on in the world these days! Bart had been roaming the rainforest as a wild animal for God knows how long! America might be under the control of some mad dictator, for all he knew!

Now Bart did laugh out loud, the panic subsiding as he felt his bear roar in pleasure deep within him. Suddenly he was focused back on his body, all those paranoid thoughts evaporating like smoke on a cold night as his orgasm approached. His body was tingling with energy, and Bart didn't give a shit whether it was dark or light, good or evil, magic or madness. The feeling of her flesh against his, his manhood inside her sex, the scent of their combined musk filling the room, the heat of their passion roiling the air . . . this was everything. It was all that mattered. As long as she was with him, they would be all right. This was how life started, wasn't it? This was the fundamental drive of life, wasn't it? The need to mate. The need to reproduce. The need to raise a family, protect that family, and do it again and again until you drop dead. It was simple. Simple and beautiful.

Bart came just as he felt the beauty of the moment wash through him, and he wasn't sure if it was because the dark magic had taken full hold or because it had been expelled from him. And as he felt himself explode in her depths like a geyser blasting its heat into the ether, he decided it didn't matter anyway. His seed was pouring into his mate, and he knew it was going to take. This train had left the station, and they were both on it.

"Oh, *fuck*!" he roared, tilting his head back as the

full force of his climax hit like a locomotive smashing through a brick wall, racking his body with sparks of ecstasy as his balls seized up, his cock throbbed inside her, his body shooting every drop of his hot semen deep into her warm valley, flooding her until he felt his own thick discharge roll down his slick shaft and drip off his balls even as he kept pouring more into her.

"Oh, God, Bart," she groaned, her face almost down against the sandstone floor as she raised her ass and spread her thighs so wide it looked like an angel spreading its wings. "Oh, God, I'm overflowing! I'm . . . I'm . . . oh, *shit!*"

Bart gritted his teeth, his eyes rolling up in his head as he felt her warm hands reach beneath them and cup his balls, massaging them as if she was coaxing even more of his seed out. He could feel himself jerk and thrash as his orgasm kept climbing, his semen kept coming out, his balls seemingly pushing out an endless supply as his mate tightened her pussy around his cock like she was milking him dry.

He collapsed on top of Bis after what seemed like minutes of continuously unloading into her, and he could barely breathe as he brought all of his weight down onto her soft body. His heart pounded like a war-drum, and he could hear her heart beat in time with his—still in time with his, always in time with his.

They lay like that for what seemed like forever, but then finally he felt her try to turn beneath him.

"I think I need to breathe now," she said, her voice muffled because Bart was smothering her with his broadness, crushing her with his weight. "Can you perhaps roll off me? Just so I can get some oxygen. I'd like to not die, you know."

Bart sighed as he rolled off her, grinning as he landed hard on the sandstone floor right by her side. One look in her eyes and his heart almost exploded with joy, because he saw that the natural light brown was back, as if the darkness was gone, like perhaps it had never been there! Had he imagined all of that? Was it just his own fear of the darkness that he suspected was inside him? The release of guilt for what he'd done when his bear had been running wild over the years, rampaging as it sought out a connection with its fated mate? Was their first mating a culmination of years of frustration, a release of all that self-hatred and guilt as his animal and human finally came into balance?

Not exactly, whispered his bear. *Yes, there is a balance that we have reached now that we are with our mate. But there is something else out of balance. It might not be clear now. Dark magic works in secret, silent, sly ways. It ebbs and flows like the tide, sometimes receding, sometimes advancing. But it is there, and it will come to fruition when she bears our children and our protective*

*instincts become all-consuming, when there is nothing
more important than our mate and our cubs.*

"When she *bears* our children?" Bart said, chuckling
like a dumb beast as he cupped Bis's face and gave her
a long, deep kiss. He held his lips against hers, rolling his tongue in her warm mouth as he tasted her.

"What's that about children?" she murmured,
breaking from the kiss, her eyelids fluttering.

"Never mind," Bart said, still grinning. "Just an inside joke."

Bis frowned, her mouth finally twisting into a half
smile as she shrugged and sighed. She took three long
breaths, blinking several times as she ran her hands
down her naked sides, touching the insides of her
thighs and then wincing.

"Did I hurt you?" Bart said, concern whipping
through him as his eyes went wide. Now he remembered how hard he'd been going at her, how damned
out of control he really was as he took his mate. "Oh,
shit, I did, didn't I? It was too much, too soon, wasn't
it? Too much for you to take."

"No, it's not that," she said, smiling as her brown
face went flush. "I can take you just fine. Well, most
of you, anyway. I'm just . . . well, look." She raised her
right hand and showed him how wet it was with his
discharge. "I'm just overflowing," she said, blinking
again as he saw the embarrassment wash across her.

Bart grinned as he felt relief knowing that he hadn't

hurt her. He kissed her quickly on her lips, and then he grabbed her hand and pushed it down between her legs. "That needs to go back in, Miss Bis," he said sternly. "I would like a hundred cubs from this first mating, and so it all needs to stay inside."

Bis giggled, pulling her hand away and then slamming it against his chest, leaving a sticky patch on his massive pectorals. "I think there's more than enough in me, thank you very much." She scrunched her face up, looking away as if listening for something inside her. "Oh, and the first set will be kittens, not bears."

"They will still be cubs," Bart said, shrugging as he frowned at the rapidly drying patch of his own semen on his chest. "You're a big cat, remember. Tiny big cats are called cubs, not kittens."

"Oh, so now *you're* an expert in zoology?" she teased.

"Just in *your* zoology," Bart grunted, running his finger down her naked left breast, circling her dark red nipple until it perked up as if standing at attention. "Soon your boobs are going to get big as they fill with milk. I can hardly wait."

Bis laughed, swatting his hand away. "I think they're big enough already!"

"No such thing," Bart said, leaning over and gently sucking her nipple as she gasped and then leaned back. "I bet you were a popular teacher."

"Wait, *what*?!" she squealed, grabbing his hair and

pulling his head away from her nipple. "OK, that's just
. . . wrong. Ohmygod, that is *so* wrong! You must have
been a sick, twisted schoolboy!"

Bart looked up at her and grinned. "You have no
idea, Miss Bis," he whispered. "Now, have you caught
your breath? Because I'm ready to go again. Ready to
teach the teacher something about her body."

Bis blinked as she stared at him. "Um, I don't think
so. My body is still in shock from what you just did
to me. Glorious, delightful, wonderful shock, but still
shock. I don't think I can . . . wait, Bart, don't. Listen,
just give me a minute. Bart. Bart? *Bart!*"

14

"Oh, Bart," she groaned as he mounted her once more, this time from the front, his eyes locked with hers as he held her wrists down firmly above her head, sucking each of her nipples until they stood pert and hard, glistening with her mate's saliva.

She raised her knees and spread wide for him, groaning again as she felt him enter her, his girth opening her cavern walls wide, his length probing deep into her secret valley, which was still full and wet from Bart's previous explosion. Slowly he began to thrust, his neck straining from the ecstasy she could see in his eyes, and Bis almost cried as her mind was flooded with images of the two of them together, raising children, teaching their young ones about the world, about themselves, about what it meant to be a Shifter in a world that was not yet ready to accept them.

What *does* it mean to be a Shifter in this world, she wondered, burying her hands in Bart's thick short hair, rubbing his neck from behind, clawing at his back as he slowly began to pump harder into her, his eyes still locked in on hers. She could sense the animal in him, but this second mating had a different feel to it. That desperate, primal, raw madness of the first mating had been satisfied, and it felt like they were already moving to another phase in their relationship—a relationship that had started in a cage meant for beasts, for freaks, for animals!

"Will our children be animals?" she whispered, touching his face as he moved above her, his weight feeling wonderfully heavy on top of her as he slid his warm, rough body over her soft smoothness. "How will we explain it to them? How will we explain what they are? I don't even understand it myself, Bart! And the little I do scares me!"

Her cat hissed from inside, as if to call bullshit on what Bis was saying. Bis almost laughed, a part of her realizing that even a straight-up human spent her entire life trying to understand herself, trying to raise her children right, trying to navigate through life's twists and turns. Bart didn't answer, and again

Bis's mind was filled with images of the two of them in the future.

This time, however, the images were darker, tinged with violence, tainted with suffering—the suffering of others! Bis yelped in shock as she felt that dark magic rise in her again like a living, breathing thing. It was tightening its hold, she realized as she glanced up into her mate's eyes, which were glowing with the same dark light she swore she could feel in her own core. Yes, the magic was slowly taking root, quietly and in the shadows, in a way that terrified her because it wasn't at all what she expected.

What *did* you expect, you fool? she wondered as her body began to shudder from Bart's increasingly hard thrusts. You enter into some game with a witch and expect to win? Perhaps that was her game to begin with! To get you to offer yourself and your mate as hostages in return for some form of freedom to raise your children. Perhaps Magda's dark magic had been working on you from the start! Perhaps the trick was to get you to *choose* to accept it, to give it access to your very soul!

Bart came just as the thought came, and Bis screamed in shock as she felt his heat pour into her depths even as the tentacles of the witch's dark magic tightened around her insides like a beast with no name. Tears rolled down her round cheeks as she saw her mate tense up with the ecstasy of his release, and although she tried to stop it, suddenly she was coming too, her climax rising up from her core like the head of a snake, its hiss sounding no different from her animal's hiss in that moment, almost like another transformation had just happened, another internal shift, a movement brought about by choice and not nature.

"Damn, that was good," Bart groaned as he collapsed on top of her, panting as his cock still throbbed inside her. "So damned good, Bis. You're so warm inside. So perfect inside. I want to stay inside you forever. I think I will, in fact."

Bis smiled but she couldn't speak, her body still convulsing from the orgasm that still flowed through her along with the magic. She stroked his hair as he breathed heavy against her bare neck. She knew he was hers: Her mate, her fate, her lover, her man. She'd do anything for him, to have his children, to raise them with him by her side, protecting his family. That was the motivation behind her choice, wasn't it? So how could it be wrong? Why did it scare her? It was the most natural, honest drive in the world, wasn't it?

"We're going to be fine," she whispered, more to herself than Bart, who in some way seemed unaffected by the magic even through she swore she'd seen that dark light in his eyes. "We're going to be just fine," she whispered again, smiling as she felt a sudden wave of relief flow through her.

And just like that she was happy again, her smile full and beaming, her mind free of those awful images of darkness and violence. Just then she noticed the sun was rising, its red glow slowly emerging in the East, its rays gently lighting the walls of their empty prison in the desert.

She blinked as the sun warmed the air, bathed the room in its happy light. But then she frowned, turning her head side to side as she tried to figure out what the hell had just happened.

"Bart," she said, tapping his broad back as a mixture of shock and delight ripped through her. "Bart!"

He just grunted, grinding his hips against hers and kissing her neck. His cock was still inside her, and clearly the man had no intention of moving his weight off her body. So she grabbed his thick hair and yanked as hard as she could.

"Ouch!" he roared, raising his head and glaring at her. "What the hell?"

"*That* the hell!" Bis said, almost mumbling as she clumsily pointed past him, to their left and right, their north and south, above and below. "The cage! It's gone! It's gone, Bart! We're free! We're free!"

15

"It's a trap," Bart said, his voice soft but stern. He was on full alert now, every instinct of both bear and soldier being called to the forefront. He took his mate's hand and held tight. "Stay behind me. And be prepared to Change. We might need to fight, and you'll need the strength of your animal."

He sensed Bis nod beside him, her hand tight in his grip. He wanted to Change into his bear right then, barrel his way through the wooden door which wouldn't stand a chance against his animal's muscled fury. His bear's sense of smell would lead him right to Murad and Magda, and he could kill them with a lazy swipe of his massive paw. Then he'd lumber back into this room rubbing his belly, shrugging and grinning like a well-fed monster, the flesh and bones of the Sheikh and the witch already half digested! Yeah, that was a good plan. Why overthink it?! Cage gone. Turn into bear. Kill everyone. Eat them. Live happily ever after with mate and cubs. Fuck, yeah, that was a good plan!

He felt his body begin to tense up at the impending Change, and he leaned his head back as his neck strained with the energy of his bear. He felt his grip on Bis's hand loosen as his own fists turned into paws the size of wrecking balls, and a moment later he was down on all fours, roaring in delight as his bear took over.

He turned to Bis, about to tell her to stay behind him, perhaps just stay in this room until he was back. But it was too late. Bis was gone, and Bart almost fell flat on his belly when he saw what she'd turned into:

A black leopard, thick and muscled, its dark sheen peppered by deep black spots. He gasped as he stared into her eyes, seeing his mate in there, his fated mate, his destined lover, the woman who was going to carry his children, the woman he somehow knew was already pregnant with his seed.

"Oh, shit, you're beautiful, Bis," he growled, leaning in and touching her with his snout. "A black leopard! I've never seen one of your kind! Very rare. Very powerful. Damn, you are one fine looking pussy!"

He jumped back as she swatted at him, her moves so quick he felt the claws slash the air like knives. "Whoa!" he shouted, chuckling as he saw some of his fur float through the air where her razor-sharp claws had gotten him. "Claws in, please! I've got enough scars."

"Sorry," Bis said, her cat's mouth opening wide like she was testing the range of her jaws. "I . . . I'm not used to this. I'm not . . . wait, did you say *leopard*? A *black* leopard? There's no such thing! Is there? I mean, I've never heard of a black leopard. Isn't that just a panther? Or a jaguar?"

"No," said Bart, circling her as he admired the perfection of her animal, its muscular haunches, thick neck, powerful thighs and forelegs, long tail that snaked back and forth like it was sensing everything around them. "Different animals, all of them. Wait, you didn't know what animal you were before I just told you?"

Bis shook her head as she turned in place, her cat's eyes warily tracking Bart's slow circles around her. "No!" she said. "I was too scared of what I was. And all my Changes before now just sort of happened. I didn't know what I was doing. I barely remembered anything when I Changed back to a human. And I certainly didn't look in a mirror!"

Bart sighed and shook his head. "Well, we'll find you a mirror in this castle. But first we've got some hunting to do." He turned towards the door and raised himself up on his hind legs, pointing his snout up towards the ceiling and sniffing deep.

"They aren't here," came Bis's voice from behind him. "I don't smell them. There aren't even any guards in the building. Just rats."

"Rats, huh?" Bart said, sniffing the air currents again and then dropping back down on all fours when he realized she was right. "Well, that's a cat's job, ain't it? Catching rats?"

Bis snarled at him, and Bart laughed as he prepared to back away from her lightning-quick swipe. They circled each other in the empty room as the sun shone through the open balconies on either end, and Bart felt the spark between the two animals as they swiped at each other playfully.

"Let's go, Pussycat," he teased. "Let's see what you got."

"I could take out your eyes before you even saw me move," she hissed, her long black tail raised up as she turned with him.

"I don't need my eyes," Bart said, shrugging as he sniffed the air and moved his ears. "I can smell a rose from a hundred miles away, hear a butterfly drying its wings on the other side of the planet."

Bis snorted with laughter, and Bart chuckled as they hissed and growled at each other, a beautiful sense of play making the atmosphere crackle with electricity. Again they traded hisses and growls, snarls and swipes, and Bart was soon roaring with delight as he decided that hell, maybe they *were* free! Maybe that magic trick hadn't worked and Magda and Murad had just given up! Maybe the bond between fated mates had its own magic, magic so powerful that dark magic couldn't break through!

With another roar of delight Bart pawed at his mate, and she swiped at him again as they ran around the room like puppies at play, Bis's black leopard almost bouncing off the walls as Bart's bear lumbered after her, knocking bits of stone from the old castle walls when he failed to catch his playmate. Around and around they went as the sun moved through the sky, neither of them tiring, neither of them noticing the time pass, neither of them noticing the sound of the door slowly creaking open, neither of them noticing the dark shadow that filled the doorway.

But then Bart smelled its scent, and he whirled around as every hair on his thick neck went rigid, his bear rising up on hind legs and standing in front of its mate in a protective stance, ready to fight, ready to kill, ready to destroy.

It took a moment for Bart's eyes to focus on the dark figure standing in the doorway, but just a moment. Just a moment to recognize its scent, to remember its red glowing eyes, to remember its name.

"Caleb!" he snarled, as much in surprise as anger.

"You treacherous piece of wolfshit. I'll kill you. I'll fucking *kill* you!"

16

Bis watched in horror as her mate leapt at the wolf Shifter standing in the doorway like a messenger from hell itself. She could feel its dark energy, smell it on the wolf's matted gray fur, see it in the beast's glowing red eyes—eyes that were the same red as Magda's cloak. Immediately she knew the wolf was under the witch's power in a way that neither she nor Bart were.

"The wolf is a familiar," she gasped, not sure if the knowledge was coming from some fairytale she'd read or somewhere else. "Magda's familiar! Which means it's a vehicle for her power! Magda can use her power through the wolf! Bart, stop! Don't—"

But it was too late, because the bear was already in mid-flight by the time Bis processed what was happening. She watched as the wolf's eyes glowed bright red, and then she screamed when she saw her mate crumple to the floor like he'd gone head-first into an invisible wall! The wolf had repelled Bart's attack like it was nothing, and now Bis felt her muscular haunches coil as she leapt forward to help her mate even though she knew it was pointless.

She felt the air getting sucked out of her as the wolf directed its dark gaze at her, and a moment later she was on the sandstone floor alongside her mate, feeling like she'd just taken a punch to the head and perhaps the gut at the same time!

"Don't be stupid, Kitty-cat," snarled the wolf as Bis gasped for air. "We're all on the same side now." He narrowed his eyes at Bart, who was struggling to his feet to prepare for another attack. "Just like the old days, right, Butterball? Except I'm in charge now. Not that damned dragon, who could barely control himself, let alone a monster like you."

"What did you do, Caleb?" Bart growled, pawing at the floor as he bared his shining white teeth at the wolf. "To me. To my mate. To yourself?"

"The same thing you two did," replied the wolf, holding his ground in the doorway like a guard-dog. "I made a deal. That's how dark magic works, Butterball. You make a deal. You two made a deal, didn't you?"

Bis blinked as she slowly found her balance and stood. Her legs were shaky, her head was pounding, her mind swirling. "Yes," she said to the wolf, not sure where she was finding the clarity to utter complete sentences. She could feel the witch's magic holding both her and Bart in place, like it was even more powerful when conducted through the wolf. "Yes, we made a deal. We made a deal because the alternative was to give up our children to those two. We made a dark deal, but we did it for the right reasons. What's your excuse?"

The wolf blinked, focusing its deadly red gaze at Bis, and she screamed in pain as she felt her insides burn with the animal's rage. She heard Bart roar as he tried in vain to attack the wolf again, and she screamed again at her own powerlessness. But then the wolf blinked once more, freeing her from whatever it was doing with the witch's magic, and Bis gasped as she caught her breath.

I got to the wolf, she realized as she glanced at Bart and blinked slowly as if to tell him she was OK, that he needed to hold back his rage, that they were in the witch's power, at the mercy of Magda's familiar. They weren't going to be able to fight the wolf in this state, on these terms. They'd made a deal, and the only way out was to make good on their end of the bargain.

"Yes, we made a deal," said Bis again, her voice firm as if she was suddenly certain she'd done the right thing, that this was going to work out just fine. "And we'll deliver on it."

The wolf growled deep in its throat, eyeing the two of them as if sizing them up. Was the witch watching all this through the wolf's eyes? Bis had no idea. Best to assume that Magda could see and hear everything. It might even play to their advantage.

Bis frowned as once again she realized she was thinking clearly, as herself, as Bismeeta. The dark magic hadn't suddenly transformed her into a totally different person. It was working subtly, from the inside out, using what was already inside Bis to work its power. This game would have to be played with herself as much as with the witch, Bis knew.

"So Magda and Murad are gone," she said finally when she saw that Bart had calmed down once he realized she was all right. "Why?"

The wolf shrugged, its long jaws hanging open in a grin. "Their work with you is done for now. You've entered into the deal, and now nature will take its course. The bear's seed is in you, and in a few months you will give birth to whatever monstrosities were conceived from your union."

"Why are you talking like you're some wise old man, you dumb hound?" snarled Bart, snapping his teeth at the wolf. "Turn off your witch's magic and let's go at it like men. I'll remind you where you came from, you rabid dog."

"I come from the same place you do, Butterball," said the wolf. "The military. The oldest and most glorious occupation of man. And I'm still in the same place, just with a different army. My own army."

"A one-wolf army," snorted Bart. "Very scary."

"You aren't scared?" whispered the wolf, glancing at Bis and then back at Bart. "You want me to fry her insides again? See what it does to your unborn children? Maybe they'll grow horns or something!"

"No!" shouted Bis, not so much because she was scared of feeling pain as much as the sudden knowledge that Bart's seed was inside her and she needed to protect herself, protect their union, protect what she was certain was already growing in her womb. She felt that dark magic coil and tighten inside her as if acknowledging the deal she'd made, whispering that she'd get to keep her kids if she and Bart delivered on their part of the bargain—whatever that was. "What do you want? What do we need to do?"

"He wants us to join his little wolf army," Bart grunted, narrowing his eyes at Caleb as his bear strained against the magic holding him back. "Isn't that right? Sure. Let's go, brother. Who are we fighting? The Russians? The Chinese? The Arabs? Aliens?"

Caleb the wolf chuckled, the sound resembling a cackle. "We'll leave those wars up to John Benson, mate. This is about something bigger, Bart. It's about giving Shifters a place in the world. Giving their lives meaning."

"What the hell are you talking about?" growled the bear. "Murad hates Shifters! He hates that part of himself! Hell, he makes the witch use her magic to stop his dragon from coming out!"

"It's not all about Murad," snorted the wolf, his long gray tail moving through the air like a snake. "The witch is using him as much as he's using her. She'll let his dragon come out when it's time."

Bart grunted. "So you're saying the witch controls his dragon? That means she controls him, right? Whether he knows it or not!"

"How could he *not* know it?" Bis said. "Murad might be crazy, but he's not stupid. If he knows that the witch's magic is the only thing keeping his dragon from going on some apocalyptic rampage, then he also knows that Magda has the power to unleash that dragon just by turning off her magic."

Caleb shook his head. "Dark magic isn't just a switch that can go on and off. You already know that, don't you? You feel it, don't you? Dark magic works from the inside. Its power comes from the dark emotions that live inside every creature—human, animal, and everything in between. Murad and Magda made their own deal, and so long as Murad keeps his end of the bargain, the witch is compelled to use her dark magic to keep his dragon locked inside. It's a give and take. A negotiation. A dance."

Bis blinked and swallowed, sensing the truth in the

wolf's words. She glanced over at Bart, frowning as she wondered why Bart didn't seem to be displaying the same understanding of how the witch's magic was working on them. But then she looked back at Caleb and it suddenly came to her.

It's because there are two sides to Bart, two parts of his personality and needs that the dark magic needs to harness to take full hold of him, she realized in a flash of terrifying insight. With me it's clear: Once I'm mated and pregnant, my animal and I have just one focus—the children. A woman spends nine months carrying a child, and so her own safety, her own body, her own protection means everything. That's nature. That's evolution. That's God and the divine at work. But for Bart it's more than that, isn't it? His primary need is to protect his mate and his young, yes. But it's also to provide for them, it's also to deal with the world around his family, find his place amongst his tribe, his pack, his brothers. That's why the witch left us here alone with Caleb! They know Caleb is the only one who can give life to that side of Bart which had been lost during the years he'd spent alone. Caleb's the only one who can open up that other need that lives in all men, the need to bond with his brothers, his tribe, his buddies—open it up so the dark magic can seep in and use those powerful masculine emotions to gain a complete hold over him.

Oh God, that's it, isn't it! Murad and Magda are

crazy, but they're frighteningly intelligent too. This is what's happening, and they know that you have no choice but to let it happen, Bis realized as she watched the bear and the wolf face off. That's part of the deal. Hell, that *is* the deal!

17

"**W**hat's the deal with this talk about finding a place for the Shifters?" Bart said as the wolf and the bear locked gazes across the threshold of the doorway. "That's what John Benson said he was trying to do, and look how it turned out."

"That's because Benson isn't a Shifter. He didn't understand us, didn't understand our needs, our strengths, our power. He thought the military would get us in line, inject some discipline into our animals, and then he'd be able to use us to do all kinds of Black Ops shit all over the globe," Caleb said. "But we're wild animals at heart, Bart. We can gain control over our animals, but in the end we're still wild beasts when we

Change! All this tiptoeing around doing covert operations just doesn't work for our kind! We need to be up front and center, on the front lines of the battlefield, letting our animals run rampage over the enemy, ripping out hearts and tearing off limbs! Benson wanted to turn us into spies, when our true strength lies in just plowing straight ahead and destroying the enemy! We aren't precision surgical instruments, Butterball. We're goddamn sledgehammers!"

Bart grinned as he felt a rush of energy go through him as Caleb's words resonated with something deep inside him. Shit, the wolf was right, wasn't he? That operation was doomed from the start thanks to Benson's idealistic fantasy about sending Shifter teams into delicate situations like hostage rescue. You don't send a bear to do a snake's job! You send in the bear when you want shit broken! Boom! Crash! Done!

"All right, maybe you're right about Benson. And about us," Bart said, his massive body relaxing as he felt he could recognize his old buddy Caleb finally. The wolf's eyes weren't glowing that bright red anymore—though in all fairness, Bart knew his bear was red-green color-blind when Changed. Still, the wolf was connecting to something inside him, and as long as Bart kept talking, his mate was safe from that damned witch's magic fire or whatever the hell had caused Bis to scream in pain earlier.

Bart swallowed hard as he tried to fight back the

instinct to kill whoever or whatever had caused pain to his mate, put his unborn children in danger. The only way he could calm down was to tell his bear that no matter what, he was going to kill Caleb and Magda at the end of it. It took a few moments of heavy breathing, but finally Bart was able to settle down enough to keep talking.

"But even if you're right about Benson not using us the right way," he said, "at least he was an American patriot. You can doubt Benson's methods, but you can't doubt his motives. He cared about America and its values. Hell, he cared about *us*, Caleb! He protected us even after we fucked up that operation! We'd both be dead right now if he hadn't stepped in and protected us long enough for us to disappear!"

Caleb shrugged. "I don't disagree. Hey, I'm not saying Benson is suddenly the enemy here! In fact I'm saying the opposite: He was a friend, and he wanted to give Shifters a way to focus their animalistic energy. That's exactly what I think we can do here while building Murad's army!"

Bart took a long, slow breath as he stared down at his paws. He extended his sharp black claws, sighing as he acknowledged that there was too much raw primal instinct in a Shifter's animal to expect them to spend their lives sipping tea and playing video games or whatever the hell it was that normal humans did all day. There would always need to be an outlet for that primal energy, that need to run wild, to run rampage, to fight, to kill, to feed, to . . . to *live*!

"So you want me to help you build an army for Adam Drake's insane dad," Bart said slowly. "We're gonna be military recruiters? Set up a booth at a college student union and park our furry asses on plastic chairs as we sign up volunteers who check a box that says, *Yes, I do occasionally turn into an animal and destroy things*?"

"Something like that," said the wolf. "You in?"

Bart snorted, looking down at himself and wondering if he could move. Nope. Still frozen in place. Shit, who knew magic actually worked so well?!

"Do I have a choice?" he said, glancing over at Bis, who was standing quietly beside him, a beautiful black leopard with the brown eyes of his mate. "Though if you *ever* hurt her again I will—"

"He won't hurt me again because he won't need to," Bis said, cutting him off so quickly Bart turned to her in surprise. Bis glared at him for a moment and then looked at Caleb. "We'll do what we said, which is to help Murad and Magda carry out whatever plans they have. We understand that the witch's magic is powerful enough to keep us in a cage or freeze us in place, and it's powerful enough to perhaps hurt our children even before they're born. But since dark magic relies on a deal and we never got a chance to talk details with the witch, let's just clear things up, shall we?"

Caleb's eyes glowed red, and Bart blinked as he swore he saw the witch's eyes somewhere in there, like Magda was looking through the wolf's eyes— the wolf who was now her familiar. How the hell had that happened, anyway? What kind of deal did Caleb the loner wolf cut with the red witch?! What could he possibly want that she had to offer him in a deal?!

"Go on," said the wolf. "What do you want cleared up?"

"Our children," said Bis, her voice smooth and silky as if she was trying to sound calm when inside she was a ball of nerves. "We made a deal because we believed our children would be taken from us and enslaved or whatever. So if Bart helps you build this Shifter army, our children will never leave our side, correct?"

The wolf nodded. "Correct. Any other questions?"

"Yes," said Bis. "What happens once this army is built? Once the children are born? Do we get to leave?"

The wolf let out a low growl through its half-open jaws. "Once you see what we're planning, you may not *want* to leave. I told you we were doing something big. And you care about making a difference, don't you? You'd like to see a world where everyone just gets along, wouldn't you?"

"And that's what the crazy Sheikh and the dark witch are planning? To make the world a better place? A return to the Garden of Eden?" Bart muttered through a smirk. "I thought I was the dumb one in the crew, but you're racing ahead of me if you believe that!"

Caleb's jaw opened wide in a hideous grin. "Funny you should mention the Garden of Eden. That's from Genesis, the first book of the Old Testament, isn't it?"

"Do I look like I read the Bible?" growled Bart.

"It is the first book," said Bis, interrupting again, her brown eyes shining with interest. "It's also the first story in the Muslim Quran. What about it?"

"Well, Genesis is the first book. What's the last book?" whispered the wolf, cocking its gray head at Bis, still grinning.

Bis blinked, and then she gasped. "The Book of Revelation," she said softly. "The end of the world. The apocalypse."

"The end of the world. Exactly," said the wolf as a chill ran through Bart. "And before every new beginning there needs to be an end, doesn't there? A cleansing. A purging. Removing the old to make way for the new. The new, Bart. That's us, baby. Shifters. The next evolution of the species. Humans are an outdated model, and the Sheikh's army is going to phase them out." He chuckled, saliva dripping down his long fangs, making his black whiskers glisten in the sunlight. "Now do you understand why we're all on the same side in this thing? Because soon there isn't gonna *be* another side."

Bart stared at the wolf, his bear's narrow eyes widening so much it made his head hurt. "What have they done to you, Caleb?" he whispered, even as the wolf's words seemed to resonate with something inside him, just like they'd done earlier. "You can't possibly believe in something like that! We're soldiers, Caleb! American soldiers! This is treason! Goddamn *treason*! And that's ignoring how freakin' *stupid* this plan is to begin with! We're humans too, you moron!"

"Are we?" said Caleb, glancing at Bis and then back at him. "Look at her. Look at us. Claws, fur, fangs, and tails. Wanna go to brunch like this? Swing by a Starbucks? Bart, we've been rejected by human society our entire lives, and that's not gonna change. People don't change their minds, don't change their prejudices. People just die, and then a new society emerges. The Sheikh is a nutcase, but hell, look at the nutcases running the world nowadays! Half of them are as insane as Murad and twice as dangerous! Look at the maniacs we were fighting while working for Benson!"

"At least with Benson we were doing our duty as soldiers, as patriots, as Americans," Bart said, breathing deep as he tried to make sense of it all—tried to make sense of the nagging feeling that maybe Caleb was right, maybe the world was so messed up and crazy that the only solution was a plan crazy enough to turn it all upside down, to start over! Hell, his own parents had tried to "cure" him and his baby sister of the Shifter "disease"! Caleb was right: They were monsters. They were never going to be accepted into mainstream society. They had to create a new society. And how better to do that than by burning it all down so the new could rise from the ashes of the old! Circle of life, right? Or some shit like that!

Bart felt a strange energy flow through him as he looked into the wolf's eyes. He was puzzled, and he swatted at his snout with his front paw and grunted. Was this the dark magic taking hold in him— taking hold through Caleb's words? Was this how dark magic worked, by making you *choose* to follow a dark path, to make it seem like the dark path actually made some sense?

He glanced at his mate, feeling her gaze upon him. He wanted to talk to her, ask her if he was insane for feeling what he was feeling, if they had all gone crazy here. But one look in her eyes told him that she was waiting for him to make his choice, to enter into this game of life or death with her. What had she told him when they opened themselves up to the witch's dark magic? Hadn't she said that this was their only choice, that either they spend their lives in a cage, trapped by the witch's magic, forced to hand over their babies every year or they take the risk of stepping forward and saying, "All right, you win. We'll go along with your plan for our own selfish motives."

She believes there will be a way out, whispered his bear. *But first you have to go all in. Play this game until*

*your children are born, and then the game will change
again. Have some faith in your mate, in your fate, in yourself. In a way you are doing what John Benson trained
you to do. Be a spy. Go undercover. Go so deep undercover that you risk losing yourself, you risk truly becoming
one with the enemy. That is the risk the greatest spies
take when they embed themselves with the enemy. The
only way to convince the enemy that you are on their side
is to actually be on their side, to truly understand their
plans, their goals, their ambitions.*

Bart could feel the turmoil rage through his body.
He wanted to trust his bear, but then he remembered that when the hell did his bear ever make so
much sense?! Hell, his bear couldn't be trusted with
shit! His bear cared for nothing but mating and protecting its young! Oh, and going on rampages! Hell,
no! This was dark magic, wasn't it! And it had taken
over his bear, which was now working against him
from the inside!

Bart stomped his feet in frustration as he tried to
figure out what to do. But then he realized that there
was nothing he *could* do! Either way he was trapped
by the witch's magic! Either he stayed frozen in place
like a fool, or he accepted the dark part of him that
wanted to head out under the open skies with Caleb
and find other Shifters who were looking for a place
in this world—find them and offer them a place in a
new world, a new society, a new age.

"How will we find these other Shifters?" he finally
said, lowering his head and exhaling hard through

his snout. "Even Benson could only find a handful of us. We're just gonna roam the Earth and sniff the air like morons?"

Caleb grinned, his eyes flashing blue—the midnight blue that was Caleb's natural color. It sent a spark of energy through Bart, and for a moment he wondered if this might be fun. Maybe he was overthinking all this crap. All they were going to do right now was find other Shifters and help them, right? Nobody had asked him to start killing innocent civilians or seize territory or anything insane like that. Not yet, at least.

"With a snout the size of yours, sniffing the air might actually work, Butterball," said Caleb. "But we'll call that Plan B for now."

"What's Plan A?" said Bis, who'd been quietly listening all this while, as if she understood that this was Bart's part of the game, Bart's time to choose his path. "Put up a billboard in downtown London?"

Caleb's eyes flashed his natural blue again as he laughed. "Something like that." He looked down at his furry paws and then sighed. "I'll show you, but we'll need to Change back to human form. It's hard to open the Facebook app on my iPhone without any thumbs."

18

"A Facebook ad?" Bis said in disbelief as she pulled her white robe closer around her body and stared at the two shirtless men hunched over an iPhone. "This is a joke, correct?"

Caleb turned his head halfway and grinned at her before looking back at the phone and swiping through. He was tall and lean, with a closely cropped buzzcut and ragged brown stubble. His eyes were a startling blue, but cold like the ocean. He looked strong and confident, and Bis wondered again how he'd become a witch's familiar, what deal he'd made with Magda. Or did Caleb really believe in the Sheikh's mad plan of bringing about the apocalypse so the world could start over with Shifters at the top of the food chain?

Do I believe in this plan, she wondered as she watched the two men, her mate and his military buddy, both of them broad-backed and shirtless, their bare torsos covered with a mixture of scars and tattoos. Bis could see that being with Caleb had awakened a side of Bart that had perhaps been lost to him in those years of solitude when he'd roamed the rainforest as a bear. Bears were pack animals, just like wolves. They needed to form bonds with creatures other than their mates. Bis herself didn't really feel that need, and as her leopard stirred within her, she understood that it was because leopards were mostly solitary creatures, happy with just their mates and cubs. Was that why she'd never felt any deep need to have close friends? Who knew.

Some of what Caleb said *does* make sense, Bis thought as she folded her arms across her chest and strolled across the sandstone floor. They were in a different room now—one with actual furniture! The furniture was old, spartan, utilitarian—not quite what she'd expected from a mad Sheikh's royal palace. But then she remembered that this was a prison, not a palace. It was just that she and her mate were now willing prisoners.

Could we even escape if we wanted to, she wondered as she stood by the open balcony and glanced out across the rolling sand dunes of the open desert. They were hundreds of feet above the Earth. Certainly they couldn't leap out and expect to land without breaking something—even if they were in animal form. Though maybe it was possible, she thought as she remembered those scars on Bart, how he'd told her that Shifters healed fast, that even bullets felt like pinpricks to him. Leopards were used to heights, weren't they? She might survive a jump from this height! Should she try?! What was stopping her?! There were no guards! She was walking freely around the room! What was stopping her?!

She blinked as she felt a strange tightening in her breasts, and she frowned as she placed a hand on her belly. She cocked her head and then gasped in shock: Something kicked at her from the inside!

Impossible, she thought in a panic. It's only been a few hours since we mated. There's no way. Absolutely no way!

She held her breath and waited for another kick, but there was nothing. It was her imagination, she decided. Just her body answering the question of why she wasn't going to run. She was safe in this castle. She was safe with her mate. She even felt safe with Caleb for some reason. Her animal wasn't going to let her leave while she was pregnant. It had decided she was safe here, and nothing mattered more than her safety while she was pregnant.

So I'm pregnant, Bis thought as she turned away from the window and looked over at Bart. She smiled as a warmth rose up in her along with images of little Barts running around her, screaming for Mommy, howling for Daddy. She let those images flow through her imagination as she stroked her round belly like it was holding something precious. I'm pregnant with Shifter babies, and they're going to be born into a world that won't accept them, a world that will call them monsters, freaks, demons! Is that what I want for my children? Isn't it my responsibility to help build a world that will accept my children, a society that won't call them freaks or monsters?

Maybe the mad Sheikh's plan *isn't* so mad, she thought as she shuddered from the memories of bombs exploding all over Syria and the Middle East. Or at least no madder than what's already happening in the world. Isn't that why everyone is killing each other in the first place? To rebuild the world in their own image, to rebuild society in a way that they believe is best for their own children?

A part of her knew that she was insane for even thinking that bringing about the apocalypse somehow made sense, but that part of her seemed small and insignificant as she absentmindedly rubbed her belly and paced the room. By the time she walked back over to the men, she had a smile on her face, a smile that she somehow knew would scare her if she were looking in a mirror.

"So we run these ads all over Facebook," Caleb was saying as she focused in on the men. "To most people, it'll just seem like a joke or a hoax. They'll just ignore it, and then Facebook will stop showing those ads to those people. Eventually the ads will get to the right people. Our people."

Bis blinked and shook her head as if to clear it. She leaned in close and snorted when she saw the text of the ad on Caleb's screen:

"The Shifting Sands Agency?" she said. "What the hell is that?"

"That's our cover organization," said Caleb. "We can't run ads that say *Are You a Shifter? Cool! Come Join our Shifter Army in the Desert*. But we can run ads that target Shifters subliminally. Like this one. Look."

"Come Join the Shifting Sands Agency," Bis read from the screen. She rolled her eyes as she looked at the graphic: A muscle-bound soldier with a tiger emerging from behind. "This doesn't even tell you what the Shifting Sands Agency is! Who the hell is going to click on these ads? Someone looking for testosterone supplements? You guys are morons. Here, let me take over. You want subliminal messaging? Here you go."

Unleash Your Inner Animal, she typed after thinking for a moment.

Release Your Secret Beast, came the next line as the men clapped and cheered.

Awaken Your Bacon, she wrote as the men roared with laughter.

"OK, the last one does sound like an erectile dysfunction drug," she said with a chuckle as she deleted it. "But you get the idea. This will hit home with Shifters who are trying to understand what they are, where they might fit in, if there are others like them roaming the Earth." She paused. "Others like us."

19
<u>SIX MONTHS LATER</u>

"**T**hey're nothing like us," Bis said as she stood at the balcony of what had become her chambers in the isolated gray castle deep in the Middle Eastern desert. She rubbed her massively pregnant belly as she narrowed her eyes and watched Caleb the wolf inspect the line of recruits, the first wave of the Shifter army.

"They are a bit rough around the edges," said Bart, slipping his arm around her waist as he joined her at the balcony. "No control over their animals. Some of them close to feral. Others terrified and confused over what they are, what they're supposed to be."

"What *are* they supposed to be, Bart?" Bis asked

softly, placing her hand over his and tensing up as she felt her babies kick from the inside. She knew it was more than one in there. Maybe twins, perhaps triplets, possibly more.

Bart shrugged, his face hardening as he stared out over the ragged lines of Shifters trying in vain to stand still as Caleb barked out orders, snapping and growling as he padded along the hard-packed sand of the castle's courtyard. "They're supposed to be soldiers, Bis. Warriors." He took a breath and swallowed, turning to her, his eyes narrowed. "Killers."

"Killers," Bis repeated, smiling tightly and raising her eyebrows. "Is that what soldiers are? Is that the *only* thing that makes a soldier what he is?"

Bart grunted, slowly exhaling as he turned back to the scene in the courtyard. "No," he finally said. "A soldier has values, a mission, a cause. Discipline, self-control, self-restraint." He snorted and shrugged. "Which is why I sucked at it."

"Did you? Yes, you lost control in that ill-fated hostage operation. But look at you now, Bart! You're steady and balanced! You can Change back and forth at will. And when was the last time you went on a rampage that you couldn't control?"

Bart grinned, his face glowing as he pulled her close and kissed her forehead. "Well, that's because ever since my Pussycat killed every rat in the castle, I haven't had anything to hunt!"

Bis giggled as she felt her mate's big hand slide

down the center of her back and rest firmly on the round of her bottom—which she swore had become bigger as her belly expanded. She snuggled up to him as they watched Caleb in wolf form angrily bark out orders to the motley group of Shifters standing in a disorderly line in the sand. It reminded her of trying to get her schoolchildren lined up for prayer and assembly in the mornings back in Damascus—a hopeless task even at the best of times!

"These so-called soldiers aren't going to be hunting anything soon either," Bis said, shaking her head when she saw two silverback gorilla shifters start punching each other like it was nothing, both of them laughing as they swung their massive fists for sport. The other Shifters were gathering around and cheering like fans at a wrestling match, and Bis couldn't help but smile at the strange sight of animals ranging from gorillas to foxes howling in languages ranging from Farsi to French! It was like a scene from an Enid Blyton fairy-tale—a twisted, gnarled version, of course!

"Soldiers don't hunt," Bart said firmly, holding her close, his eyes narrowing as he surveyed the scene of semi-chaos out on the training ground. "But you're right. These aren't soldiers. They're no better than schoolchildren. They're just learning about themselves, about their animals, about what a Shapeshifter is. It's a perfect environment for them, actually. The open desert. They can unleash the energy of their animals on each other, and since they're all Shifters, no one is gonna get hurt." He grunted as one of the gorillas took a resounding crack to the jaw and went down with a roar as Caleb jumped in to stop the fight before it got out of hand. "Well, not too bad, anyway."

Bis winced, touching her belly as she watched the strange scene out there. The gorilla who'd taken the punch was back on his feet, beating his chest, clearly ready for more. But Caleb was having none of it, and Bis sighed when she saw the wolf glance angrily towards Bart as if to say, "Come help me, you big lug! Control these animals! We're building an army here, not a group of ruffians!"

"I should probably go out there," Bart said with a grin, shrugging comically at Caleb and finally nodding. "Caleb isn't cut out for this. He was a Navy SEAL. They worked in small, close-knit teams, and that's where Caleb shines. He's not cut out to be a general of a thousand-strong army, let alone train them to fall in line!"

"Neither are you, clearly," Bis teased, stepping away from her mate as she felt the energy of his bear roll through him, his Change imminent. She loved watching him Change to his bear, and she couldn't wait until she gave birth, until her babies went through their first Change, grew into what they were born to be.

"What the hell does that mean?" Bart growled, raising an eyebrow. "Did you just insult your mate? I'm the man here, Pussycat. You will show me respect. I'm the father of your children, the general of an army! Hear me roar!"

"Bears don't roar," Bis said with a giggle, a rush of warmth flowing through her as she watched Bart finally Change into his big, beautiful bear. Its fur had regained its deep brown sheen, its claws smooth and clean once again. Bis herself had been Changing back and forth at will over the past six months, and she was now so comfortable in her leopard-skin (as she called it) that it all seemed natural, seamless, meant-to-be.

A chill cut through the warmth as she felt the lingering unease that often came to her when she stepped back and thought about their situation. It still seemed strange as hell that she was thinking as "herself" and not some deranged person under a witch's spell. Yes, she understood how dark magic worked, but still it felt weird to be happy, to feel safe and protected, her body filled with warmth and love! Had the magic worn off? Or was it hiding in the background, sowing its seeds deep into her subconscious, setting her up for a bigger fall?

The conflict and uncertainty had ebbed and flowed within her over the past six months as her belly grow large, her breasts filled with milk, her cheeks grew dark brown and rosy from the days spent on the open verandahs with her mate. She'd asked herself again and again if she was just in denial, if she was blocking out the gruesome reality of the situation from pure near-sighted selfishness, the selfishness of her animal who cared for nothing but the immediate safety of its cubs. After all, her mate was building an army that was going to bring about the end of the world! And she was standing by his side, one hand on her pregnant belly, watching from the wings like an evil queen!

She watched as her mate bounded out onto the training field in the courtyard below, barreling into one of the gorillas headfirst as the other Shifters screeched and howled in delight. Caleb barked and snapped his jaws as Bart rumbled in play with the other Shifters.

"This isn't helping!" Caleb growled as Bart knocked over one of the gorillas, caught the other one in a friendly headlock, and kicked at a laughing hyena Shifter that was playfully snapping at his heels. "You're supposed to be setting an example for these undisciplined monsters, not joining in their stupid games! We're trying to build an army here, not a goddamn circus!"

Bart turned around and did a clumsy forward-roll, throwing up a cloud of sand that sprayed Caleb right in the snout and eyes. And then Caleb was in it, baring his teeth and leaping at Bart with a howl of delight, the two so-called leaders of the army rolling around like puppies at play!

Bis laughed and clapped her hands as she watched

the ridiculous scene out on the battleground. Again that feeling of lightness and warmth went through her, and she realized it was because this group was so far from becoming a fearsome army that it seemed almost impossible that they might someday run rampage over cities, nations, the entire world!

Why is that, she wondered as she looked at her mate out there, the big bear wrestling with his military buddy as the other Shifters pawed the ground, snapped their jaws, whipped the air into a frenzy with their tails. There was no doubt these other Shifters had all the same instincts to hunt, feed, kill. And they'd all been drawn together by those ridiculous ads touting the *Shifting Sands Agency*, which was still some undefined organization based out in the Middle Eastern desert! She couldn't help feeling an underlying sense of fate, of some bigger picture being formed—a picture she couldn't quite see yet.

"Why?" she asked Bart as he finally came bounding back into the castle after his play-fight with Caleb.

"Why what?" said Bart, panting as he came up to her and pushed his massive snout against her, sniffing her scent and growling in satisfaction. "Why do you smell so good? Is that the question?"

Bis giggled as she pushed the bear's nose away from her armpits. "You're disgusting. No, I mean why is this . . . so much . . . so much *fun*?! Why are we so happy, Bart? It's scaring me! We're supposed to be prisoners, under a spell of dark magic, fulfilling our part of a deal with a witch! But we're happy and healthy, deep in love, about to become parents! You're having a blast out there with your buddies, and you're clearly not making any effort to actually train these Shifters to be warriors!"

"Not making any effort . . ." Bart said slowly, his snout widening into a grin. "So you noticed? Is it that obvious?"

Bis cocked her head and placed her hands on her wide hips. "Um, if anything, you're making those young Shifters even more undisciplined! What I don't understand is why Caleb is tolerating it. Why he hasn't . . . I don't know . . . hasn't reported us to the witch or something."

Bart shrugged. "Because Caleb is enjoying himself too," he said. "Yes, he's a loner, but he's still a wolf, a pack animal. I think just being ourselves, enjoying being animals without having to deal with society or any of that crap . . . Bis, I think it's bringing him out of that witch's spell, just like it has for us."

Bis frowned as she studied her mate's face. "You think we're not under Magda's spell anymore?" she asked cautiously.

"I don't know if we ever were," said Bart. "Yes, I felt something six months ago. And yes, I remember almost buying in to Caleb's argument of building a new society from the ashes of the old or some crap like that. But that just seems so ridiculous now, the delusion of a madman, the dreams of a clown!"

"Mad clowns can still be dangerous," Bis said, forcing a smile as she watched Bart slowly Change back to human form. Caleb had dismissed the troops—if they could even be called that—and the courtyard was empty now, the desert sun low on the horizon, a gentle breeze making her white gown swirl around her bare ankles, hug her thick thighs. "This reminds me of a dark fairy tale, where the witch or demon comes back after years and demands that its victims make good on their deal. It's trickery, lulling your victim into a false sense of security."

Bart was all man now, naked and bronzed by the sun, his massive chest heaving from the exertion of wrestling with his Shifter buddies. He was grinning, and she could feel the energy in him. It was clean, pure, intensely masculine energy, and Bis reminded herself that this was good for Bart, that horsing around with his buddies was filling a void in his soul, healing what was broken in him just like finding his mate had filled a missing piece in the powerful bear Shifter. Maybe he was right. Maybe their love had conquered the darkness. Maybe Magda and Murad would never come back. Maybe Caleb would be freed from his spell. Maybe it was all going to be perfect. It was all going to work out. Maybe this *was* their happily ever after!

He kissed her just as the thought entered her mind,

and she gasped as Bart's strong hands closed tight on her breasts, his thick fingers pinching her nipples so hard she squealed in shocked delight.

"Ouch!" she mumbled as he twisted her nipples and ferociously kissed her lips again, driving his tongue deep into her mouth and swirling it around like he wanted to taste her, drink from her, eat her up. "Careful with those. They're not just playthings for you. Soon they're going to be reserved for our babies."

"The little brats will have to fight Daddy for access to these," Bart growled as he pushed her against the sandstone edge of the balcony and lowered his face to her breasts, sucking on her left nipple right through her white satin gown. "I was here first, and Daddy feeds before the babies."

"You are *sick*," she whispered, tilting her head back and staring up at the dark blue sky above them. She gasped as she felt her mate suck on her right nipple, his thumb and forefinger clamping down on the left one and plucking at it. She could feel her gown getting soaked with his saliva, and she finally reached down to grab his hair and pull him away so she could get her gown off before he ripped it like he'd done with so many others.

But Bart was pressing his face tight into her breasts, his mouth clamped tight over her right nipple, his eyes closed in ecstasy as he sucked so hard she almost came right then and there.

"Wait, why is my gown so wet?" she groaned as

Bart pulled his face away so he could give her other nipple some attention. "What's all that white stuff on your lips and face? Ya Allah, is that . . . is that my . . . my *milk*?"

Bart licked his lips and grinned wide. "Creamy and fresh," he growled, ripping her gown down the middle, all the way down to the bottom until it just hung on her like a tattered cloak.

Her breasts popped out, heavy and large, her dark red nipples glistening with her milk. She wore no bra or underwear, since she'd been captured naked from that pastry shop in Damascus—not that her regular bra or panties would fit her anyway: her boobs had become too big, and even her hips and ass seemed to have expanded in preparation for bearing her cubs.

"Oh, shit," she muttered, her eyes going wide and then rolling back in her head as her mate hungrily drank from her, his right hand sliding between her thighs and cupping her mound firmly, rubbing her roughly, his middle finger lining up against her dripping slit, his thumb pressing hard on her throbbing clit. "This is sick, Bart. Twisted. I think we should . . . I think we should . . . oh, oh, oh . . . oh, *God*!"

20

She came all over his hand just as a hot jet of her milk shot into Bart's mouth, and he almost went blind with ecstasy as he smelled his mate's sex, felt the wetness from her cunt cool against his hand as the heat from her cream warmed his insides. He was so hard he thought he might come without her even touching him, and he pumped her heavy breasts as he drank from her like a filthy schoolboy, his fingers parting her slit from beneath as he prepared to drive his cock up into his mate.

She came again as he finally rose up and slid his shaft all the way inside, doing it as slow as he could out of concern for her pregnancy. He'd been taking her from the rear over the past few months, usually preparing her gently and lovingly before letting himself go wild and blast his load deep into her anus. But now he wanted to feel her pussy from the inside, feel her warmth, her wetness, her valley. Maybe he could add one more cub to the brood by coming in her right now. Hell, it was possible, he was so damned aroused!

He looked down at her shuddering body, groaning at the sight of her brown breasts pressed up against his hard body, the white milk running in streaks like rivers down her skin, her pregnant belly looking perfect and round from his viewpoint above her.

"I need more," he growled, pulling out of her and going down on his knees so he could suck her boobs again. "All of it. All of you."

"Uh-huh," she mumbled, nodding and then arching her neck back as he licked the milk off her belly, running his tongue up beneath her breasts before circling each nipple and finally closing his lips and sucking, moving his mouth back and forth from one nipple to the other as he pumped her breasts until she was flowing free and hard.

He cupped the big globes of her ass, parting her buttcheeks and driving two fingers into her rear hole as she grinded up into him. He was full with her milk, and with a gasp he pulled back, leaned lower, and began to eat her pussy with all the animal in him.

"Oh, *Bart!*" she howled as she came all over his face, her hips pushing into him as he curled two fingers inside her asshole while driving his tongue as deep into her vagina as he could. Her slit was parted all the way, his nose so deep inside her that he was almost dizzy from the lack of oxygen.

He kept going, taking heaving breaths of her sex, bringing her all the way through her orgasm until he felt her seize up and then relax with a shuddering sigh, her body almost crumpling on top of him from the wildness of her climax.

Slowly he lowered her to the smooth sandstone floor of the verandah, every muscle in his body pumping with energy as he laid her down before him, her curves bare and exposed beneath the darkening desert sky. Although his cock was throbbing for a release, Bart felt more satisfied than he'd ever been, than he'd ever imagined he *could* be!

"I love you, Bis," he whispered, stroking her smooth round cheeks as she smiled up at him through glassy eyes. "I can't even describe the love I feel for you right now, for what we have, for what we're going to have."

She nodded as he placed his big hands over her pregnant belly, gently rubbing her smooth brown skin as she looked down at herself. "I love you too, you big, disgusting bear," she whispered, reaching out and wiping his lips, which were sticky from her milk and her sex.

"Disgusting? Taste yourself and you'll understand why I couldn't help myself," he said.

"What? No!" she said, scrunching her face up. "Bart, no! Eww!"

Bart brought his fingers up to her nose and mouth as she closed her eyes and tried to turn her head away. But he was too strong, and finally she relented, her eyes opening wide as she allowed him to push his sticky fingers past her lips. Soon she was sucking his fingers, two at a time, her dark red lips moving back and forth over his thick fingers until Bart felt his erection yearn for some attention.

Slowly he straddled her body, one knee on either side, his fingers still in her mouth as she began to gently moan while she sucked on them. He groaned as he dragged his heavy cock up along her breasts, circling each oozing nipple until her cream coated his cockhead and shaft.

"Now taste me," he whispered as he brought his erection up to her mouth, slowly replacing his fingers with his swollen cock. "Taste me, Bis. Taste me. Suck me. Drink me."

Her eyes flickered open as her lips expanded to handle his girth, and Bart groaned in pleasure as he leaned forward until his balls were hanging beneath her chin, his cock slowly pushing down her throat as she opened up for him.

"Oh, hell, that feels good," he growled as she dragged her lips past his cockhead, rolled her tongue around his shaft, opened her throat for his length. "Damn, you're getting good at this, Miss Bis!"

Bis pulled her mouth away and glared up at him, her face going red with embarrassment. She gripped his cock, holding him back as she frowned playfully and narrowed her eyes. "Did I have a choice? You've spent the last six months shoving yourself into every opening I have, I should remind you."

Bart smiled tightly, his neck straining with arousal as he tried to force his cock back into her mouth. "I'll make a new opening if you don't take me back in, woman," he growled, reaching down and slowly massaging her throat. "Come on now. Open up. Open up for your mate. It's feeding time."

"You are *so* sick!" she squealed, opening her mouth in shock at his comment. But then she couldn't speak, because Bart took advantage of the opening to ram his cock back into her mouth, grinning as her eyes went wide as she fought her gag reflex.

"Open your throat like I showed you," he whispered as the ecstasy rose up in him. "Breathe through your nose. And keep your teeth tucked behind your lips. I don't need any more bite-marks on my . . . oh, that's it, you got it, that's good, that's . . . oh, fuck, babe. Oh, *fuck!*"

He roared as he came with such violence that he jerked his hips forward, and then he was fucking her in the mouth as she held her throat open for his load, her warm hands cupping his balls and milking him just like he'd milked her, his mate swallowing his cream just like he'd swallowed hers.

He came for what seemed like hours, his grunts of ecstasy mixing with the sucking sounds coming from her lips clamped tightly around his thick, glistening shaft. The feeling of pouring himself into her warm mouth was divine, and Bart roared as he finished, his heavy hands pounding the sandstone floor near her head as he pumped and flexed one last time, squeezing out a massive last load before pulling out of her mouth and collapsing, making sure not to land on her pregnant belly.

They lay there in silence, naked and panting, each of them coated with the other's juices, animals and humans all in one. And as Bart experienced that sense of clarity that happens for a few moments after a man shoots his load, he thought he understood what Bis had said earlier about the strange tranquility that had defined their lives over the past six months, the entire time of their pregnancy. It really did feel like there was something brewing, something they were missing, like they were being lulled into believing they'd won, that the magic hadn't taken hold, that they were free even though they were sinking into a trap.

As the feeling of unease only climbed, Bart turned his head and glanced down at his mate's round belly, frowning as he wondered what the witch's game was, what she wanted.

"You don't think . . ." he started to say, turning on his side and placing his hand on Bis's belly, on his unborn children. That protective instinct fired through his veins as his bear growled in the background, and in that moment he was reminded that there was an animal in him, a wildness in him, an instinct that would allow him to do anything for his mate, his children, his family.

"No," said Bis firmly, turning her head and looking into his eyes as if she'd been thinking the same thing. "The witch said our children would stay with us. That was the deal. She won't break her end of the deal, or else the deal crumbles and the spell is broken."

"What spell?" Bart said as the frustration rose. "I think it's already broken, Bis. I have no intention of preparing these Shifters to go to war—certainly not to become efficient killing machines that can be commanded and controlled. We're in love. We're happy. Maybe we just make a run for it, babe. I don't think Caleb can stop us. Like I said earlier, maybe the witch's magic has worn off or something. Maybe Adam's dad finally Changed into a mad dragon and killed the witch! We haven't seen them in six months!"

"We can't run," Bis said quietly. "Because our part of the deal was that we wouldn't run, that we'd stay here and do what they asked. Maybe the witch is dead or her powers are weakened. But we have no idea, and if we break our side of the deal, then all bets are off. We might be back in a cage before the morning, our children snatched from us the moment they leave my womb. We need to play this out, Bart. We need to play it out."

21

<u>THREE MONTHS LATER</u>

"**A**re they out yet?!" Bis screamed, her legs spreading wide as she tried again to push. She'd been pushing for hours, and she'd already counted two babies before her vision had blurred and her senses had shattered from the pain.

"One more," said Bart, reaching up and dabbing the sweat from her brow, petting her hair feverishly as he stared down at her from above. "Triplets, Bis! Three beautiful bear cubs! Here she comes, Bis! Hold on, babe. Keep pushing!"

Bis gasped as she writhed and then pushed. Her head was on Bart's broad lap, and she looked down past her spread-out legs at the three silent midwives who were assisting with the delivery. The women had shown up the previous night as if by magic. They were dressed in black robes and head-coverings, their heads bowed in servitude, never making eye contact with Bis or Bart. Their arrival had alarmed Bis, and she'd wanted to send them away. She wasn't sure if they'd been sent to take her babies away!

But the moment she went into labor, she knew she'd need their help. Sure, animals gave birth in the wild, but she didn't want to take any chances. The health and safety of her cubs were more important than anything else, and she had to take the chance that these midwives—who were undoubtedly sent by the witch—would not break the witch's vow that the children would not leave their parents' side.

With a final scream she felt her third child slide out, and the third midwife swiftly caught the child, lifted it up, and cut the cord with a clean curved knife of shining steel. The silent woman placed the newborn on a clean towel, quickly tying the end of the cord with professional skill, the result looking like a little rose nestled on top of the little one's belly button. Then all three midwives solemnly washed and wiped each child before turning their attention to the mother.

Bis blinked as the three women cleaned her up with

gentle but cold hands, and she looked down at their bowed heads as her body slowly relaxed, the tension oozing out of her as the women worked. Soon she was clean and dry, just like her babies, and then the anxiety rose as she wondered what the midwives were going to do next.

She felt Bart's crossed legs tense up beneath her head, like he was prepared for anything, perhaps prepared to Change into a bear and kill these three women if they made any move to harm or take his children.

"Wait," she whispered as the midwives each picked up a baby and faced the parents. "Hold on, Bart. Just wait."

Bart was still tense, but he waited, and Bis smiled in relief as the midwives came forward and carefully placed the three children on their mother's breast, where they could hear her heart beat. Then they stood, bowed their heads again, and quietly walked away, leaving not even their scent in the air.

Neither she nor Bart could speak as the tension finally drained from them, leaving nothing but joy. Three bundles of joy, pure and natural, perfect and clean. Bart slowly laid Bis's head on a rolled up towel and carefully snuggled up to his mate and cubs, his big arms pulling his family into him as Bis gasped from the feeling of five hearts beating in unison, beating as one, one family, one life-force, one reason to live.

One reason to live, but also one reason to kill, Bis

thought as she felt her mate's kiss and felt her leopard stir inside, purr inside, the animal reminding her of what it meant to be a beast with newborns. She imagined herself Changing into that deadly black leopard, its shining claws ready to rip anyone and anything to shreds if they dared come between her and her cubs, her mate destroying anything that even *looked* at them funny.

But then she relaxed again and enjoyed the moment, smiling when she realized that they were alone here, safe for now, that no one was going to look at them funny.

22

<u>TWO MONTHS LATER</u>

"**A** little funny-looking, but they're cute, I suppose," said Caleb with a wolfish grin that nonetheless had a certain warmth to it.

Bart raised an eyebrow as he looked down at the three baby girls in his big arms, all of them wide-eyed and curious, staring at Uncle Caleb with no fear in their eyes. Indeed, after keeping his distance from the parents and newborns for almost a month as if out of a healthy respect for the ruthlessly protective natural instincts of mother and father, Caleb had finally knocked on the door to the private chambers and asked permission to see the kids.

Bis had been reluctant, but finally they'd agreed when Caleb assured them he would only be around the triplets in human form, never as a wolf. Besides, what real choice did they have? Sure, the witch still hadn't showed up or asked for anything; but after those silent midwives had shown up precisely in time for the birth, it was obvious Magda was alive and at least some of her magic was still strong. Perhaps all of her magic.

"You call my children funny-looking again and I'll bite your ears off," Bart growled at Caleb even though his eyes twinkled with mirth. "Then we'll see who's funny looking."

Even Bis smiled as Caleb stood by the doorway, not making any move to come closer—certainly not to pick up the children. The wolf did seem genuinely curious at the sight of the babies, and Bart almost wondered if there was a paternal instinct buried somewhere in that lone wolf's cold heart.

Caleb cleared his throat and shifted on his feet, rubbing his buzzed head and then his unruly stubble as if he wasn't sure what to say or do.

"What now?" Bis finally asked, cutting through the awkward silence that had fallen across the room.

"What do you mean?" Caleb asked, still rubbing his stubble, blinking several times. His eyes were still that cool midnight blue, but as Bart stared, he swore he saw a flicker of red in them—red like he hadn't seen in months.

"We've made good on our end of the deal," Bart said, slowly handing off the kids one by one to Bis in case he needed to Change, in case he needed to fight, in case he needed to kill. Caleb was his friend, and indeed they'd recaptured their bond over the months they'd spent together while Bis was pregnant. But nothing came between his bear and its family. Nothing and no one. It was time to take his family and leave, and neither wolf nor witch was going to stop him.

"Have you?" said Caleb, that redness slowly beginning to glow in his eyes as Bis hugged her children tight and began to move behind Bart. "Where's our army, Bart?"

Bart shrugged. "I gave it my best effort. That was the deal."

"The deal was to help me build an army, not a goddamn circus!" snapped Caleb, and Bart frowned as he heard the anxiety in the wolf's voice. Caleb was usually cold as ice, but clearly something was worrying him. Did it have something to do with whatever hold the witch had on him? Something to do with whatever dark deal Caleb had cut with Magda? "You tried to play us, tried to throw the game. That means the deal is broken, you dumb bear."

"Good," Bart growled as he summoned his bear, which he could now do at will, now that his animal and human had been brought back into balance because he'd found his mate and done what nature intended. "Because here's my new offer, you mangy mongrel."

The Change blasted through him as he leapt through the air, his bear exploding out of the man in mid-air, his fangs bared, every claw out and ready to rip the wolf to shreds and end this crap once and for all.

But then suddenly time stood still, advancing in snippets, like a series of photographs in his mind. He saw Caleb's eyes turn to that blazing red as they went dead, and the next moment he felt like all the air had been sucked out of his lungs. With a gasp he fell straight down to the floor with a massive thud, using all his remaining energy just to turn his head and look at his mate and his cubs—one last look before the lights went out.

23

Bis screamed as she saw her mate go down with a thud that shook the entire castle, it seemed. She almost let her leopard burst forth, claws and teeth ready to kill the wolf. But she couldn't let go of her two-month-old babies—and besides, she knew that she'd be knocked out just like Bart had been.

The witch was back.

She'd never left.

"Magda," Bis managed to stay through teeth that were gritted so hard she thought she saw sparks come out. "You're not getting them. We had a deal."

"The deal would have been broken the moment your mate decided he could trick us by making sure these Shifters could never be organized into an army," came Magda's voice from what seemed like nowhere. Bis blinked and swallowed in fear as she watched a swirling dark cloud form in the air near the doorway. It looked like a little twister, a mini dust-devil, and as it spun faster and faster suddenly the witch walked right out of it and into the room.

Bis gasped again as she tried to speak, and as she got a grip on herself, Magda's words repeated themselves in her head. "Wait," Bis muttered with a frown. "You said the deal *would have* been broken, not that it was *actually* broken!"

"I know what I said," Magda replied, raising a thin eyebrow and straightening out her perfectly straight black gown in a way that seemed oddly self-conscious for an all-powerful dark witch. Magda glanced briefly over at Caleb, who'd been standing still like a statue, his hard, muscled soldier's body tight and rippling in his shirtless state. Then she turned back to Bis. "There was no deal, because the dark magic never took hold. I thought it might—indeed, it did enter the two of you using your primal instincts to do anything for your children as an entry point." She sighed and shook her head, her dark eyes narrowing, flashing a look of what Bis swore was wistful admiration. Just for a moment though, because then that deadness was back in her eyes, and she smiled tightly. "But I underestimated how pure and clean an animal's instinct to kill in protection of their family is. It's a different kind of darkness, and my magic couldn't enter deep enough to bring you two over to our cause. No matter though. Because I had suspected it might happen. You two weren't really the prize I was after anyway. I just needed you two to mate, and since you refused to do it in captivity—which, I admit, was surprising—I offered the deal even though I suspected my magic wouldn't work. Well, at least not the way you thought it might work. I'm still going to get what I wanted."

The witch glanced at Bis's three babies, and Bis felt her heart almost explode as she tried to grip them tighter. But her arms were frozen, and although she didn't drop her children, she couldn't hold them any tighter either.

"No," Bis whispered. "You can't take them. I'll do anything. Another deal! Anything! Anything for them!"

But Magda just shook her head and smiled, and Bis felt herself almost die as her leopard tried to break through and slash the witch to ribbons. It couldn't get through, and Bis just began to wail helplessly as the witch got close and reached out her bony white arms.

Bis's vision blurred for a moment, and when her sight returned she realized that even though Magda was all the way against her and the children, the babies were still firmly in Bis's grasp. Then Bis looked down at witch's hand, and she gasped when she saw a clean glass syringe with a thin, gleaming needle made of surgical steel.

"What are you doing?" Bis managed to say as she

watched powerlessly as the witch slowly poked each child with the needle, drawing a drop of blood from each of the triplets. "What the hell are you doing, you sorceress?"

"Setting the rest of my plan into motion," whispered the witch, squinting as she carefully squirted the blood mixture into a vial. She walked to the open balcony and looked out over the open desert, raising her left hand as if testing the air currents. Then she opened the vial and held it up, muttering under her breath as she blew over the top.

Bis stared as a thin wisp of red smoke rose up from her children's blood. The smoke hung in the air for a moment, its shape looking like a ethereal dragon. Then in a flash the smoke shot out into the open desert as Magda muttered another spell before turning back to Bis with a triumphant smile on her thin face.

"The bear and wolf are able warriors and powerful soldiers," said Magda, glancing over at Caleb and then the frozen bear on the floor. "But to build an army to do what I want, you need a dragon."

Bis blinked as she tried to put all of it together: The blood, the spell, the dragon-shaped smoke in the air. Blood was a powerful component of dark magic, wasn't it? Of *all* magic, perhaps! What was special about her children's blood? How would it bring a dragon to Magda?!

"Adam Drake," she mumbled, thinking back to the dragon that Bart had talked about. The dragon she'd seen in the desert. The dragon who was mated with Bart's sister—a woman who shared Bart's blood. And Bart's blood ran strong in his children, of course. Was that the connection? Was the witch using the blood as bait, a lure, a way to bring Adam Drake to them? "But . . . but why wouldn't you just have used Bart's blood? It would still connect him to Adam Drake's mate."

"The blood of children is innocent and pure, much more powerful. It will create an unmistakable beacon for the dragon, who is undoubtedly looking for his mate's brother," said Magda. "The bear's blood alone would not be enough. It needed to be distilled, and for that you need the blood of a newborn."

"So you draw Adam Drake's dragon here. But then what?" Bis said with a frown. "You think your magic is going to work on a dragon when it doesn't work on a bear or a leopard? You think by drawing Adam Drake to us, you'll be able to capture him and get him to lead your Army of the Apocalypse?"

Magda snorted. "Adam Drake isn't the dragon I'm after, Miss Bis," she whispered, folding her arms over her slight chest.

Bis cocked her head as she tried to put Magda's words into context. What other dragon?! Then it hit her. "His father? Murad? But you already have power over Sheikh Murad's dragon, don't you?"

"I can stop him from Changing, but I can't control the dragon when it does finally Change," said the witch. "Only Murad himself can do that."

"Except he hates his dragon, denies it, suppresses it," Bis said. "So what's going to change his mind? He's a nutcase, I should remind you. Good luck injecting some sense into a madman!"

"There is one thing that will change his mind, force him to release his dragon while at the same time bringing his dragon to heel," said Magda. "The most powerful force in the world. Love. Love for his own blood."

"His son, Adam Drake?" Bis said with a snort. "From what I hear, they hate each other."

"No, not his son," said Magda, turning her head towards the open window as if she sensed something coming. "Adam Drake will never forgive his father, never reconcile with the man." She narrowed her eyes into the blue sky, and Bis followed her gaze until she could make out a speck in the distance.

At first she thought it was a bird, but then it got closer, its wings catching the sun and shining gold and green with iridescent light. It was a dragon, and it was coming in fast. Adam Drake was here. He'd come for his military buddy, for his mate's brother, for his extended family.

Bis glanced back towards Magda, but the witch was gone. Caleb was gone too, and Bart was stirring on the floor as he regained consciousness.

"My babies!" Bart roared, leaping to his feet, clearly one thing on his mind. His eyes were wide with panic, but then they relaxed with relief when he saw that his mate and children were safe, that his family was safe. "What happened, Bis? Where's that witch? And the wolf?"

"Both gone," said Bis, blinking as the dragon's huge shadow fell across the open room. She pulled her babies close and shielded them with her mate's massive body as she herself ducked down. "Oh, and you should duck too, unless you want some more scars from your buddy Adam Drake. Or should I say your brother-in-law."

"What?" growled the bear, going up on his hind legs and doing the exact opposite of what Bis told him to do just as the dragon smashed through sandstone and brick with its mighty wings. "Oh, shit. Oh, *shit*! Adam, you dumbass bird! It's me! It's *me*!"

24

"I told you it was me, you asshole!" Bart grumbled as he winced from the swelling above his eye where the dragon's wing had clipped him. He was still in bear form, his strong arms holding his three cubs securely as he dug the claws of his free paws deep into the dragon's back as they flew through the air.

"I knew it was you," replied the dragon, turning its massive head and winking at the bear. "I just wanted to remind you that I'm stronger than you, Butterball. Heard you were getting too big for your boots down in the rainforest, terrorizing squirrels and other small furry animals."

Bart chuckled as he glanced over at Bis, smiling wide when he saw her in leopard form, holding tight as she looked over to make sure her babies were safe in Daddy's arms. She hissed back, her jaws opening wide in a grin. But she stayed quiet, like something was on her mind.

"Well, the squirrels get mighty big down in South America," Bart said, digging his claws into his buddy's scaled back and laughing again. "They even have those flying squirrels. Bet they could give you a run for your money, Flyboy."

The dragon laughed, and the two of them traded quips and insults as the dragon flew through the air. Soon they were past the desert, and the dragon began its descent towards a teardro-shaped sea that was a startling midnight blue.

"Is that the Caspian Sea?" Bis said after riding in silence, her ears pinned back as the dragon descended.

"Yes," said Adam. He gestured with his head. "My lair is down there."

Bart chuckled, turning to Bis and rolling his eyes. "Adam calls his home a *lair*, in case you didn't know. Pretentious pretty-boy. Born with a silver spoon in his mouth." He turned back to the dragon, raising his voice above the screaming wind. "Oh, we met your dad, by the way. He's a fucking nutcase! Now I understand your issues a lot better!"

"I can drop you off here if you keep that up," rumbled the dragon. "Last time I checked, bears don't swim."

"OK, please hand me my children before you boys

go swimming!" Bis shrieked from Bart's left. "And you, Mister Dragon: I'll make sure I tell your wife that you put her nieces in danger."

"Wait, you got *married*?" Bart shouted as the dragon leveled off and slowly began to glide in for a landing on what appeared to be a massive castle made of gleaming white rock built atop a magnificent mountain on an island of lush green. "I guess my invitation got lost in the mail, huh?"

Adam shrugged, the motion making all of them rise up as the dragon's muscles tensed and released. "What can I tell ya? Can't trust the government these days. Sorry, bud." He looked over at the two of them and winked. "You'll still invite me to your wedding, right?"

Bart frowned as he looked over at Bis. "Oh, yeah. Are we doing that?"

Bis widened her eyes and swiped at him with one paw. "Is that your form of a proposal? You are a true romantic. I'm moved to tears."

"Thanks a lot for bringing it up, asshole," Bart muttered to Adam as he shook his head. "I don't even have a ring."

"I'll take care of the ring," the dragon whispered, turning in the air and flying past one of the castle's towers. "That's the best man's duty, anyway."

Bart blinked in shock as the dragon glided past the open window. Inside was a heap of jewels and precious stones: a straight-up vault of goddamn treasure! A hoard! A stash! Bart couldn't even speak, he was so stunned. "Um, yeah," he finally whispered back. "The ring *is* the best man's responsibility." He looked over at Bis, raising his voice as the dragon rose up towards the massive flat terrace between the spires of the castle and turned to come in for a landing. "Hear that, honey? We're getting married! Did you hear me, Bis? Bis? Hey, Bis?"

25

Bis had been listening to the boys banter back and forth, and although she'd been enjoying it along with the ride through the clouds, a part of her had been going over the witch's last words just before Adam's arrival had ended their conversation.

Love, the witch had said. The most powerful force in the universe. Strange for a dark witch to talk like that, wasn't it? Love . . . a blood connection . . . the primal instinct to bond with your children.

Your children, she thought as she glanced at Adam Drake, this massive dragon who hated his father as much as the mad Sheikh seemed to hate his son. Or your . . . grandchildren?

The realization hit her in a whirlwind of panic as the dragon finally landed its powerful feet on the flat open terrace. "Adam," she said as the answer suddenly came to her spinning mind. The answer that sending out the blood signal wasn't so much to draw Adam Drake to come rescue them as much as it was to draw Adam Drake away from his lair!

Away from his mate.

Away from his children.

Away from Murad's grandchildren.

Bis shot a look at her mate. "Don't let him leave, Bart. Don't let the dragon leave. Here. Give me the kids and hold on to your friend. Do not let him leave. No matter what you need to do, Bart!"

"What's going on?" said Bart, handing over the kids and leaping off the dragon's back as he watched the dragon whip its neck back and forth like it was going into a frenzy. "What the hell is going on, Bis?"

"There!" said Bis, holding her babies close and pointing over towards the far end of the terrace, where she could see a figure slumped on the white tiles. "It's your sister, Bart. Stay with the dragon! I'll go to her. She's all right. They wouldn't kill her. They—"

"*Ash!*" roared the dragon, its voice like thunder, the reverberations almost knocking Bis off her feet. A flash of blue flame whipped out from its nostrils, and then suddenly the dragon was a man, naked and bronze, running like a golden flash towards his fallen mate. "No! No!*No!*"

26

"The wolf," said Ash, her eyelids fluttering as she glanced up at Adam. Then she frowned when she realized there were other people present. She blinked, reaching out and touching Bart's face. They were all in human form now, all of them gathered around Ash, who seemed to be coming out of the same spell that had knocked Bart out earlier. "Oh, God! Bart?! Is that . . . is it really . . . oh, God, I don't understand . . . I can't even . . . Adam, they took . . . they took our . . ."

Her head went limp against Adam's chest before she could finish the sentence. But she didn't need to finish the sentence. It was clear what had happened. The witch had gotten them—gotten *all* of them with her trickery. She'd twisted all of them around, drawn the dragon from its lair, made it easy for her wolf-familiar to seize the dragon babies and bring them to Grandpa—even though Grandpa might not be expecting it! Magda was the puppet-master, the dark mistress pulling all the strings!

She lost focus for a moment, and when she looked back, she saw that Adam had stood up straight and was shaking. His arms were spread out wide, his eyes closed tight, eyelids fluttering.

"I can see a path through the skies," he muttered. "Straight to my children. I found them when they were still in Ash's womb. You think I won't be able to fly straight to them now that they're in danger? You goddamn morons. I won't even bother to chew your bones before I eat you."

"No!" Bis screamed. "Bart, you need to stop him from Changing."

Bart nodded, leaping to his feet, his bear exploding from his body even as Bis saw the wings start to emerge from Adam's back. She knew that if Adam Changed before Bart got to him, he'd just knock the bear aside and take off to get his kids. And God knows what would happen then! Perhaps that was Magda's intention: If Adam got there breathing fire and hell bent on destruction, maybe it would force Murad to unleash his own dragon! Hell, that alone might bring about the Apocalypse: Two dragons in an airborne firefight! Who would be able to stop that?

"You can," she whispered to her mate, a bear more powerful than almost anything she'd ever seen. "My man can stop him. Do it, Bart. Do what you do best."

With a roar the bear was on him, enveloping Adam with a bear hug so strong that the dragon's wings were forced back inside! Adam shouted in anger, but the bear was too strong, its bear-hug so powerful that even the dragon couldn't explode from inside the man! Bis could see that Bart was using strength that he didn't know he had, didn't know he was capable of using, strength that perhaps he wouldn't have access to in any other situation. Strength powered by love, a love for a brother, a love for a friend, a love for his alpha.

"Let me go, you goddamn bear!" Adam roared, wisps of smoke rising from his ears and nostrils as he struggled against the massive bear. "I have to go to my children! You're supposed to help me, not stop me! How do you not understand that?!"

"I do understand it!" Bart roared back, baring his teeth as he fought to stay in control. "But you can't just fly in there breathing fire! Think about what happened the last time we tried to rescue hostages! This might be exactly what the witch *wants* you to do! We need to think, Adam! We need to plan this out!"

"Think? *Think*?!" Adam howled, his struggles decreasing as the bear began to win him over with his sheer strength. "*You're* telling me we need to think? You're the goddamn reason that first hostage rescue blew up in our faces! You killed everyone including the damned hostages!"

"Exactly!" Bart howled back. "So I know exactly how it feels to make a mistake where people get killed! And I can't let you make that same mistake, Adam! Especially not when the hostages are your own children!"

That seemed to hit home, and Bis could tell that Adam had finally calmed down enough to realize that flying in there and potentially going against his father's dragon could put his children in even more danger.

"All right," Adam said through clenched teeth. "I said *all right*! Now let me go before you crush me like an egg! God-damn you got strong, you overgrown furball!"

Bart finally let him go, and Adam slumped down to the ground and crawled back over to his unconscious mate, holding her close and stroking her pretty round face. They all went silent, and Bis glanced at Adam and his mate before looking over at her own mate, who'd Changed back and was standing there naked, glistening with sweat.

Bart came over to her and his children, holding

her close as Adam whispered reassuring words to his passed-out wife before looking up.

"So what are we thinking about?" he said, his gold and green eyes blazing. Bis knew it was only a matter of time before Adam would lose his patience, turn into his dragon, and go after his kids. And this time Bart might not be able to stop him. This time she had to do it.

Her mind swirled as she surveyed the scene: Shifters and their mates. Fated mates. Born for each other. Bonded with each other.

Suddenly an image of Magda and Caleb popped into her head. She frowned as she remembered the way Magda had self-consciously straightened her gown and glanced over at Caleb as if she cared about how she looked to him, like she was attracted to him, like she cared about if he was attracted to her.

Could it be?

No, it couldn't . . . could it?

Ohmygod, *could* it?!

"Ya Allah," she muttered, the thought coming to her that it was the only thing that might explain why Caleb seemed so taken in by Magda's power. It wasn't her dark magic that had bonded him to her. It was that other kind of magic. The magic that brought fated mates together, that made fated mates willing to do anything for each other, the magic that had brought Ash and Adam together, had given herself and Bart three beautiful baby girls, a magic born of pure light, the same light that created the universe and everything in it.

The magic of love.

"Ya Allah," she said again, her heart filling with hope. "I think . . . I think . . ."

"Spit it out, Pussycat," Bart growled as he glanced over at Adam. "A bear hug isn't going to stop this dragon a second time."

Bis sighed as she took her mate's arm and smiled. "I think we've got a chance at a happy ending. A happy ending for all of us. Three happy endings instead of the End of the World."

"What do you mean by three?" said Ash, who was conscious now and had been listening.

"Caleb and Magda," Bis whispered, now almost certain she was right. "I think they're fated mates. Just like Ash was destined for the dragon and I was born for the bear, I think the witch was made for the wolf."

"Holy Mother of God," Bart muttered, staring wide-eyed at Bis and then slowly beginning to nod. He turned to Adam, who was frowning, his jaw clenched tight. Soon he started to nod too.

"It might explain how she was able to get Caleb so deep under her spell," Adam finally said, nodding again. "Your mate is smart, Bart. Good thing for you, because you're dumb as a rock."

They all chuckled a little, breaking through the overwhelming sense of despair and tension as Bis's words of hope and optimism seemed to spread amongst the group. Soon they were all nodding in agreement, and then Bart grinned wide, winking at Bis before raising one finger in the air.

"Speaking of rocks," he said, raising an eyebrow to go with the finger. "Excuse me a minute. I'll be right back."

They all frowned as Bart suddenly Changed into a bear and barreled down a stone staircase. They could hear him bounding into the depths of the castle. Then a moment of silence, followed a second later by a humongous crash.

"My vaults!" shouted Adam, racing towards the stairs and almost getting crushed by the bear coming back up, a massive diamond ring clutched in one of its paws. "Wait, how did you get in there? Those doors were supposed to hold up to a goddamn explosion!"

"All that practice fighting squirrels in South America," Bart whispered with a wink. He slapped Adam on the shoulder. "Thanks for the rock, buddy. Best man, I mean." Then he turned to his mate, Changed back to a naked, muscled, tattooed soldier once more, and went down on one knee.

"Thought I'd make this official, Pussycat," he whispered, slipping the ring onto her finger and looking up into her eyes with a seriousness that almost broke her in two. "Just in case the next episode gets us all killed. This way nobody can say we didn't get our happily ever after, yeah?"

"I think romance readers would actually call this a happy-for-now," said Bis as she dabbed her eyes and nodded out a yes to the question that Bart didn't need to ask but was asking anyway. "But we'll have to live with it for now. Until the dragon gets his kids back, and the wolf gets his witch."

Until the wolf gets his witch . . . ;)

∞

FROM THE AUTHOR

The first two couples are together, but they've still got to fight for their forevers. Are you ready for three happily-ever-afters rolled up in one mindblowing Book 3? Good, because there's a witch out there with a wolf's name written in her dark heart—whether they know it or not!

Get Witch for the Wolf now to read the heartwarming end to this first trilogy of the Curves for Shifters Series.

Oh, and if you haven't read my Curves for Sheikhs Series, you should! It's madness, drama, and over-the-top steam—just like every Annabelle Winters novel!

Finally, join my private list and you'll get five bonus scenes from my Sheikh Series right away!

Thanks for being a reader.
I love writing for you!
Anna.

∞